Daneshvar's Playhouse

Daneshvar's Playhouse
A Collection of Stories

Simin Daneshvar

translated from the Persian by Maryam Mafi

Mage Publishers
Washington, D.C.

First published in 1989 by
Mage Publishers, Inc.
1032 29th Street, N.W.
Washington, D.C. 20007
(202) 342-1642

Design by Najmieh Batmanglij

Library of Congress Cataloging-in-Publication Data
Danishvar, Simin
Daneshvar's playhouse: a collection of stories
Translated by Maryam Mafi
I. Title.
PK6561.D262A25 1989 891'.5533—dc19 89-2527

ISBN 0-934211-19-1

First Edition

Printed in the United States of America

The stories were translated from three volumes first published in Iran:
Shahri chon Behesht, Tehran 1967
Be Ky Salam Konam, Tehran 1981
Ghroub-e Jalal, Tehran 1982

"Dedicated to Dr. Wallace Stegner, my guru and inspiration."

Simin Daneshvar

". . . for Chuquk . . ."

Maryam Mafi

Contents

Vakil Bazaar

At the entrance to the Vakil bazaar, Marmar let go of the child's hand. She straightened her veil and said, "Dearest, you go ahead slowly, and I'll go buy some nuts. Be sure to walk close to the sides." She headed straight for the nutshop. When the little girl pulled her hand from her nanny's, it was wet. She dried it, rubbing it against her dress, took her doll in the same hand, and was instantly pushed forward into the bazaar by the crowd. The bazaar floor was uneven, but the girl was so preoccupied with her doll that she paid no attention to the holes she stepped in, nor did she worry about her nanny's absence. The doll, although quite ugly, was her dearest possession, and as she strolled along, she childishly promised it everything she herself wished to have. She flattered the unshapely puppet and then scolded it, imitating her mother and her nanny.

Speaking like them made her feel older, and she imagined herself to be a real mother, although she was only six.

She had begged her nanny to make her a toy for ages. The nanny had postponed the task for some time. Finally, one day, having found a couple of hours to spare, her nanny had made the doll. She had filled it with cotton from head to toe, stitched two red triangles—which were now more black than red—for the cheeks, a straight black line for the eyebrows, and two large—but lifeless—round circles with black spots in the center for the eyes. The chin was a round mark sewn with the same black thread. The arms and the legs of the doll were exactly the same size and shape, sticking out of the pillowlike body. No matter how hard the child tried to move them, she never succeeded and had eventually given up the idea.

The girl, busy with her doll and oblivious to her surroundings, passed a row of shops selling cloth. Veiled women, concealing their faces with muslim masks or face covers, squatted on short stools in front of the bazaar platforms, bargaining with shopkeepers. Brand new fabrics, stiff with starch, were spread out before the tradesmen. Some were quickly measuring the cloth with half-meter sticks while others cut the material with their large scissors. Some spoke to their customers, laughing and joking with them, while others, frowning, snapped at the women. The girl, uninterested, glanced at them and passed by. She thought, without looking back, that Nanny was not far behind and would soon be by her side. At any moment she expected her nanny to call her and give her some nuts. It didn't occur to her that her nanny could be late. She was even glad to have distanced herself from her nanny, and did not have to listen to her boring "do this, don't do that . . ." There was something about the marvelous life of this bazaar which attracted the little girl. Perhaps it was the various sounds and the commotion heard in the distance; perhaps it was the humid and stuffy afternoon air or the donkeys with their drivers and the laborers walking with their heavy loads shouting wearily in a hoarse voice: "Attention! Attention! Watch out, step aside." Or could it be the very special scents found only in a bazaar, like the smell of dampness, tobacco, mint, pepper, and turmeric or the smell of incense mixed with human sweat, blending in with every other indistinguishable aroma? But had she known that her nanny was not following behind her, the attraction of her new findings would not have mattered and she probably would have burst into tears and run away as fast as she could.

She stopped in front of a toy store near the first crossroads of the bazaar. Every time she had passed there with her nanny, the dolls in the window had winked at her. She had always wanted to stand and watch them, but her nanny had always pulled her hand and taken her away from them. She stared at the dolls, and only at the dolls, with wide eyes. What beautiful creatures! They lay in their large boxes like princesses on their beds with their eyes closed. They even had eyelashes and arched eyebrows. Their curly blond hair, the color of kernels of corn, surrounded their pretty faces. Their cheeks and chins were so fine one almost wanted to touch and caress them. How lucky they were! How well-dressed they were! Their large skirts came down below their knees; they even had socks and shoes! Their bodices were made of ruffles, lace, and ribbons. The girl wanted them so badly and felt so angry at having such a miserable doll that she almost ripped its legs apart to pull out the ugly cotton inside. She glared at her doll closely. The way it looked made her want to vomit. It had a dirty scarf around its hairless head, and its blouse and pants looked horrible. Its empty eyes only accentuated its lifeless and sad face; instead of lips it had a red dot underneath a long black stitched line which was supposed to be its nose. Its stiff arms stuck out; its legs were long like those of a dead person who had been crucified. She wondered how this dilapidated doll had occupied her for so long and why its existence had been so important to her. She wondered why she could never go to sleep at night unless she held this ugly puppet close to her, sang lullabies to it, and tucked it in a hundred times. Involuntarily she dropped the doll. It was instantly trampled by the crowd which swept the child away. She was no longer in front of the toy store. She had even lost her own doll. Only now did she begin to panic. Slowly she started to feel alone in the huge bazaar. She looked around carefully for her lost one. She felt a lump in her throat and burst into tears. She wanted to cry out, "I'm lost, I want my nanny." She even thought about going back and picking up her doll, but she knew that it was lost forever. A tremendous fear developed in her small tummy. Through her tears she looked at the people around her with a peculiar suspicion. At that point she even preferred to be deceived by someone rather than believe she was actually lost. She stopped and looked behind her, paying close attention to the ladies in black veils who were coming toward her; she was looking for her nanny. The women all looked the same, like black sacks tightly tied at the top and bottom. The only way to differentiate them was by their veils, whether they were old or new. Her nanny's veil was new; her face cover too, was clean and tidy with lace covering the eyes.

The lost child looked at all the black-veiled women with face covers, but did not find her nanny.

The nanny, however, was now sitting comfortably in the back of the nutshop. She had taken off her face cover and was playing with its cheap shiny flower broach. Her forehead was scored with a red band from the face cover's strap. The shopkeeper, brown faced, wearing a green nightcap, watched her with lustful eyes and made pointed remarks:

"Sweet sister, it looks like you've become chaste and innocent these days . . . Well, where are you living now? I heard you've gone back to your old master. How come he's taken you in again? Perhaps you've got him hooked on a potion?"

He put a cup of tea and a few lumps of sugar on a tray and pushed it in front of her. Marmar, without the slightest thought of the little girl who was wandering about, lost in the bazaar, said: "Oh, come off it. Who else would stay and work for them but me? They have six children, of all ages, running around the place from dawn to dusk. I have to watch over them every minute. Madame has nothing to do with these things; she has herself to attend to . . ." Sensuously, she took a lump of sugar, put it between her lips, and sipped her tea through it.

The nutseller, in his dirty shirt and pajama pants, was squatting in front of Marmar, mesmerized like a charmed snake. It was obvious he wanted to tease her, get her all worked up, and enjoy watching the reaction. He said: "Well, sweetheart, can't you see? They found no one else who can do their dirty work as well as you!"

Not only did the nutseller's remarks not upset Marmar, they made her want to flirt with him even more. The shopkeeper asked, "By the way, do you remember the day the mullah whipped you in front of everyone for wearing thin stockings? What a scene you made! Do you still dare to wear thin stockings?"

He burst out laughing so hard that tears rolled down his cheeks. As he laughed, his yellow, uneven teeth and his purple gums showed. Marmar remembered the day he was talking about. She remembered the mullah who had whipped her ankles—not so hard though; it had even felt pleasant, but she had screamed her head off, disturbing the peace of the entire quarter. When she finished her tea, she said:

"The bloody mullah; his own daughters are the worst. He doesn't dare say a word to them though. As soon as he steps out of the house, the girls quickly fix themselves up, wiggle their behinds voluptuously, and their father has the nerve to tell me off. Can you believe that!?"

It was apparent that Marmar could not stand the mullah or his daughters, because her neck veins had swollen and her voice quivered with jealousy and sadness.

Marmar knew that the nutseller was thoroughly enjoying their conversation and was secretly admiring her complexion, her deep dimple, and her black eyes and eyebrows.

He simply refused to show his emotions because he was so stubborn and selfish. He stood up and prepared a dish full of nuts for Marmar. Without delay, Marmar thrust her hand into the dish, took a handful, and rapidly emptied it in her mouth and said, "What tasty nuts you have!"

Meanwhile, still looking for her nanny, the girl's attention had been drawn to a rhythmic sound coming from a corner. Forgetting her fear and worries, she walked toward the sound, which was coming from a cotton-beating shop. Inside, a heap of cotton filled the entire store like a thin sheet of snow, almost blinding one's eyes. An old man with a white beard sat on the white stuff in one corner, and a younger man in long black trousers sat in another corner carding the cotton. The monotonous, yet interesting, *zim zimboo* sound of the beating engrossed the child. She was amused by the bits of cotton which flew like snowflakes around the men. They were being slowly covered by the floating white stuff as it came down. The child, for a while, enjoyed this monotonous music; she even laughed at the carder, who constantly bent up and down over his card. She had forgotten her panic and fear of being lost in this crowded bazaar. She stayed there for a few minutes. But soon even this upset her, how monotonous and boring it was. It didn't seem like it would ever end or even change. The same tune was repeated over and over again as the same cotton flew into the air. Bored and depressed, the girl walked away, only to be faced again with the endless commotion of the marketplace. For a moment she thought she would never be able to make it home. The mere thought gave her the shivers, and she started to run like mad.

She wanted to flee quickly from that place, that immense

and crowded bazaar. She could no longer stand the
deceiving marketplace with its temporary amusements, its
strangers who could not understand how lonely she was,
and how much she wished to be consoled. They went about
their own business with no notion that she was desperately
lost. Even if they did understand, they probably could not
have cared less; they only bumped into her and stepped
on her feet. She wished to leave the deceitful bazaar which
had tricked her, and find a quiet place where she could cry
her heart out. She wanted to go and find her nanny and
hide under her skirt, grab her veil so tightly that she would
never get lost again. She longed to beg her nanny never to
leave her side and never again to let go of her in the bazaar
the way she had.

The nanny, though, was totally engrossed in her own
chatting. She was now smoking a hookah, coquettishly
letting out the smoke through her nostrils and telling stories
about her past. She recalled those evenings when she had
to spread the bedding out on the roof. She would lie on the
mattresses, revealing her underarm and part of her breasts
as the son of the mullah, the same mullah who had whipped
her ankles, came up to the roof to cry out the evening
sermon with his recently broken voice. She remembered
the evening when, at sunset, she had gone to the neighbor's
roof, pretending to want a better view of the mountain.
And with her sweetest high voice she had said to the young
gentleman: "Sir, God bless you, it looks like the mountain
is pregnant. It's grown so big it seems it's going to have
twins." She remembered how he had sighed sweetly and
how she had gone on to say: "It must be the moon or the
bright shining stars that have gotten it pregnant." And the

young gentleman had said: "Woman, who are you to talk of God's creation like this? Bite your tongue!" and Marmar had known he had loved her way of talking. He was staring at the beauty mark on her upper lip and Marmar had said: "Sir's got such a lovely voice."

Marmar removed the cover of the water pipe, letting out the smoke. She blew the coals on top and rearranged the half-lit embers with her hand. She then replaced the cover and handed the water pipe back to the nutseller, saying:

"The boy would come up on the roof every day for one reason or another. In the end, he even used to come up in his pajamas, peeking down to our house, signaling me to go up. Of course, I'd play hard to get and wouldn't go, just to tease him, and to make him want me more. Finally, he could bear it no longer and went out of his mind. His thick-headed father recited all sorts of prayers and ablutions to cure him, but to no avail. His family even thought he had become possessed and tried to exorcise him. That, too, didn't work. You know why? Because his cure rested with me. So finally his family came to their senses and took me as his temporary wife. My breath cured him on the spot . . ." Marmar suddenly jumped up. "I've got to leave. I left the poor child by the entrance of the bazaar and came here. I couldn't help stopping by to say hello." The shopkeeper took her hand and pressed it firmly, saying:

"Where are you going? Take it easy. She'll be all right. Let's enjoy the few minutes we have together."

The little girl, still searching for her nanny, was filled with fear and desperation. She had now reached the first crossroads of the bazaar and was confused as to which direction to take. Should she stay where she was until her nanny showed up? Should she turn right? She knew the way home was to the right of the bazaar; but at the very end the dirt alleys became narrow and full of turns, and she was frightened of them. If she turned left, she would end up in a large square where the horse carriages waited in line, and she was always afraid of them, too. She was scared of being stepped on by the monstrous animals. Her nanny had often warned her against dogs, donkeys, and horses. She waited for a while and then chose to go straight ahead, passing through the intersection. The sight of a dervish in front of a grocery store singing "Ali, my Lord" made up her mind for her. She stood close to him and stared curiously at his long white beard, his top hat, and the basket he was carrying. The dervish walked very slowly, stopping at every other stride, saying things which the girl could not understand. He put his hand into his basket, took out a few candies, and offered them to a pot-bellied shopkeeper sitting on top of a platform next to huge sacks filled with various colorful things. The sacks, some half full, caught the girl's eye, especially the ones filled with raisins, dates, and walnuts, but she ignored the sacks containing rice, peas, chickpeas, and lentils. The only sack she could not make out was one filled with round white things; were they dried whey or a kind of candy? The dervish offered the little girl one of his candies. She hesitated, becoming scared again, and scrutinized the man. She remembered her nanny's frightening stories about the "child-snatcher." Instinctively, she concluded that the

strange person in front of her who yelled out incomprehen-
sible words and walked so slowly could be no other than
the "child-snatcher." She thought: "He could easily grab
me and put me in his basket and throw it over his shoulder
and run away." All of a sudden she became frightened and
refused the sweet and did not look at him anymore. She
quickened her stride and was soon running away . . .

The bazaar floor was full of potholes, as always, and at
the speed she was running away from the dervish, a little
boy bumped into her; before she could pull herself together
she was sprawled on the ground. Her knee hurt; once again,
she began to cry and wish for her nanny with all her might.
The boy helped her up, smiled at her, and brushed the
dust off her clothes. He examined her knee and said, "Don't
worry, it's nothing; it'll be all right. Where's your mother?"
The lost girl looked at the boy through her tears—she
smiled. All of a sudden she felt calm and thought she could
trust the little boy.

Until then, the girl had tried several times to appeal to
one of the many black-veiled women, telling them she was
lost and asking for their pity. They moved rapidly though,
and would not look at her. Now she had found the little
boy, and her tears dried up. She took his hand firmly and
told him she was lost.

And then she forgot everything; her getting lost, her
falling down, and all her fears and worries. Her face lit up.
This was the happiest and most comfortable she had felt
since she had entered the crowded bazaar. Nothing she had
come across compared to the sweet conversation she was
having with the little boy. The pleasure she had found in
watching the pretty dolls and the white-bearded dervish

had ended quickly. In the company of the little boy, though, she now found something which did away with all her apprehension and insecurity. They walked in and out of the intriguing passages and even went back some ways so the boy could show her the colorful lanterns in a grocery shop. They enjoyed looking at the sea lanterns hanging from the ceiling, the various colorful bags of tea, and the large white sugar cones; they especially liked the "Box of a Thousand Crafts" located next to the shopkeeper and the old scale in front of him. Enviously, they stared at the colorful, cleanly folded paper lanterns standing out among the rest of the things. The boy explained, "You can light the candle inside the lantern at night and show it off to the kids around the little bazaar." The girl said, "Yes, I know."

They continued their expedition. The next row of shops they passed was not interesting, so they paid no attention. The only shop which caught the girl's eye was one with multi-colored coils of silk and beautiful linens and lace and all sorts of beautiful buttons. The shopkeeper was weighing some yellow silk on a small scale. What beautiful silk it was, the color of the dolls' hair! But the boy took her away from there, and she happily followed him, having totally forgotten not only her wandering, but also her nanny.

And as for the nanny, who had followed the nutseller's advice, she was still sitting in the back of the shop and had forgotten all about the child she was supposed to be taking care of. She was telling the shopkeeper the story of her happy life at the mullah's house.

"You can't imagine how much he loved me and spoiled me. He'd tell me, 'Don't dirty your feet on these hard floors; walk on my eyes instead.' Every night when he'd come home he would bring me a handkerchief full of sweets, candies, and limes. He'd pick all the jasmine blossoms in the garden and drop them between my breasts. He'd tell me, 'My sweet nightingale, why don't you sing to me?' "

The shopkeeper quickly puffed at the hookah and said sarcastically, "Nightingale, eh?"

This made Marmar remember her mother and sisters-in-law; she recalled how she used to clean up after the ladies during the day and the mullah at night and that she was not so happy after all. True, the boy did care for her, but his mother and sisters did their best to make her miserable. It was also they who maliciously told him all kinds of lies about her, succeeding in making him lose interest in her. Every day they would go and ask for the hand of a different girl in marriage for him. They would speak about daughters of noblemen in front of her, making her look worse and worse in his eyes, whetting his appetite for a real lady.

Marmar, her train of thought broken, raised her head and bragged to the shopkeeper, "Although my husband treated me like a queen, I didn't forget my old masters. I visited them every day, took their little girls in my arms and never forgot to take them some of the presents I used to receive. My heart was with their youngest child, and I couldn't help it. You can't imagine how much I care for her; she's just like a grown-up." Again, she remembered the little girl. This time she stood up and said, "I really must get going now. The poor child is wandering about the bazaar all on her own; I have to go find her." The shopkeeper begged her to sit and convincingly said, "Where are you going again? If she was meant to reach anywhere, she's probably reached it by now."

At the same time, the lost girl walked with the boy hand-in-hand through the alleys, happy and carefree. Together they went toward a grocery shop at the second crossroads, in front of which a man was beating a rhythm on a tin can while another was making funny faces and moving his body to the rhythm. A small crowd had gathered around them and applauded. The man doing the mime was dressed in rags; his dirty black trousers were torn and patched in several places. The children stood there watching the poor and hungry pair of entertainers lightheartedly dance their time away, looking as if they had nothing on their minds other than making merry and enjoying themselves as best they could. Their eyes twinkled as they laughed hysterically, bending their bodies up and down and around. The dancing man turned around and suddenly came face-to-face with the kids. He pulled out his tongue and rolled his eyes, scaring the two, who ran away as fast as they could. Once again, the girl remembered her nanny and the fact that she was lost. She was gradually growing impatient and had started to nag; she was bored.

The boy, too, had grown impatient and didn't want to put up with the girl's whining. He frankly told her, "The bazaar is full of fun. I'm going to have a good time without a bore like you tagging along. Besides, you're always falling behind and everything scares you. I want to go and look at the toys, the fights, the weird people, the back alleys, and talk to other little girls . . ." After he had finished saying all these horrible things he left her at the third crossroads and did not even look back.

The girl, fatigued and totally lost, only wished she could find a spot to sit down and rest for awhile. But there wasn't a comfortable place in the bazaar, especially this part with narrow passages. It was filthier and more dilapidated than anywhere else. Even the shops were pitiful ruins; some were closed down and their entrances boarded up. And those that were open had nothing to interest the girl. She saw a jumble of samovar tubes, pliers, and stools hanging from one of the shop's ceilings, and wondered what all those metal things were used for. Here the roof of the bazaar was decrepit and part of it had collapsed. The girl was desperately trying to get out of there as fast as she could. She wanted to come out of the bazaar altogether. Perhaps once she could see the bright skies again, she would even find her nanny. She quickened her step, but was soon stopped as two donkeys, one behind the other, came towards her carrying loads of hay and taking up most of the passageway. She looked at the loads tied to the donkeys' backs with black ropes—they seemed awfully heavy. She looked at the donkeys; they were thin and seemed to be on the verge of collapsing. They did not even have the customary blue beads hanging from their foreheads—she always enjoyed counting those. She thought the animals would fall down any minute and the hay on their backs would fill the entire bazaar. But the beasts moved on slowly and with dignity. People had to stand aside and make way for them. After the animals had gone by, the passers-by would complacently clean their clothes, which had become covered with hay. The girl was astonished at how casually and courageously the people treated the huge beasts. She, however, was frightened; she was not sure whether she should climb a platform or squat on the floor. The beasts were getting closer. Out of nowhere, a man thrust his hand forward, took the girl's thin arm and pulled her to the side. The first donkey, with its immense and awesome load which the girl had expected to fall any minute, safely passed by. She glanced at its feet—they were long and thin and shook as they stepped in a pothole. The second donkey also passed by her without incident.

The girl was relieved and looked at the man who was now holding her hand. He was tall and thin with a rimmed hat and glasses. He had a modest appearance; but his hand was too large and rough, and the girl's hand was uncomfortably lost in it. He asked, "Where do you live? Who did you come with? Whose daughter are you?" Not waiting for her to answer, he continued, "Don't be afraid; there's nothing to worry about. I'll take you home." The girl looked him over. A childish suspicion and fear gleamed in her eyes. She said to herself, it's him; it's the same one my nanny was talking about. It's the Jew who snatches Moslem children and takes them to their quarter and kills them and makes bread with their blood . . . A sound rang in her head: It's him. It's him.

The time that had seemed endless, full of misadventure, fear, and suspicion to the little girl, had passed as quick as a wink for the nanny and the nutseller. They were completely unaware of the passage of time. Although Marmar had thought of the girl several times, the persistence of the nutseller and her own carelessness and neglect had diverted her attention from the child she was meant to look after. She had, in fact, used 'taking the child for a walk' as an excuse to get to her admirer. The man spread a silk handkerchief with red and black stripes on the ground and filled it with nuts, mostly pistachios and hazelnuts. Meanwhile, Marmar was bitterly describing the marriage of her temporary husband to the daughter of one of the town's noblemen.

"His malicious mother, whose corpse I hope to see lying in the morgue, used all kinds of magic on him to turn his love into hate. He finally dissolved our marriage contract. And then one day they borrowed a whole lot of jewelry from my first master's wife, adorned themselves like circus mules, and went to ask for the hand of the new bride. The mullah, may his turban fall around his neck and strangle him, married them himself. A few nights later, they prepared the bedroom and brought her home wrapped in a veil. I put on my veil and went and stood on the threshold of the ceremonial bedroom where the party was starting. His fat stupid mother couldn't sit still; she kept clapping her hands and jumping up and down. His moronic sisters, instead of celebrating and singing happy songs, kept reciting sermons, as if they were attending one of their father's prayer meetings. There was such chaos and tumult in the ceremonial bedroom that the dust was lifting up from the carpets. I couldn't bear it; I was on the verge of tears. The boy, smiling, looked at everyone but me; so I went to the kitchen, stuck my head in a vent hole and screamed my sighs as loud as I could. That night I cried so hard my pillow was soaked; I didn't sleep at all. As the mosque clock struck four, I was about to doze off when suddenly there was a racket of clucking and cheering, celebrating the consummation. The next morning I packed my bag and kissed my bloody mother-in-law's shoulder and told her that I was sorry if I had been a burden or if I had caused them any trouble. She offered me a two-*toman*[1] note, which I naturally refused to take. I bid them farewell and left their house. Since then I have been working for my old master. They're truly decent people. Well, I'd better go now, it's almost dinner time. I've probably given you a headache with my silly talk. Heaven knows where the poor child is now; she has probably poked her head in every single junk shop she's come across."

The shopkeeper handed her the handkerchief full of nuts. Marmar, tying her face cover, said, "You're very kind," and winked at him.

"Take care of yourself, sweetheart," said the nutseller. "You're some hot number!"

Marmar pulled up her stockings and stepped out of the shop. She asked the first person she knew if she had seen the little girl, but to no avail. A cossack officer with a turned-up moustache began to follow her by the Sun pharmacy. He touched Marmar's leg with his walking stick. Marmar turned around, pushed her face cover away, and said sweetly, "Officer, dear, don't hit me with your cane. I'm a decent lady, don't you see?" and she winked at him. The officer followed her into the bazaar. Marmar asked the various people she knew about the girl. Most of the bazaar merchants knew her well and teased her without giving her the information she sought. She passed the first crossroads and turned right. She stopped at an ice cream and sherbet

---

[1]*Toman*: One *toman* is 10 *rials*, or approximately 13 cents at the official rate of exchange. In today's black market rates, one *toman* is equivalent to one cent.

store and began chatting with the owner. The man quickly filled a cup with sherbet, sprinkled powdered sugar on top, put a small jar of orange blossom extract and a jar of lime juice on a tray, and put it in front of Marmar.

"Enjoy it," he said. "Where have you been, sweetheart? And where are you off to now?" Marmar coquettishly flirted with him a bit, had her sherbet, and carelessly walked away. Whoever she saw—friends or strangers— she'd ask about the girl, describing her clothes and the doll she carried. She'd say, "Do you know which way she went?"

The girl, her hand lost in the unfamiliar rough hand of the man, walked with him until the end of the bazaar. There, the marketplace was empty and devoid of life. It was nearly sundown. The girl could not stop thinking about the "child-snatcher" and the way he killed his child victims. She envisioned the scene of the killings. All she could see were very large knives the size of their own kitchen knife, with which her nanny skillfully chopped vegetables on the big brown cutting board. She could even hear the noise it made every time the knife landed on the wood. She imagined the knives like the swords used by the men who gathered in front of the mosque for the religious ceremony where they chanted "Hossein, my Lord" and suddenly brought the swords down onto their own heads, making blood run all over their bodies. God, she was afraid of them! Just as she was afraid of the man now holding her hand. As they reached the last exit of the bazaar, the man saluted a friend and let go of her hand so that he could get something from his pocket. The girl hesitated for a second and then ran for her life. Her heart beating rapidly, she did not dare look behind her; she could not have cared less about the potholes. With incredible speed, she got herself out of the bazaar, turned right, and found herself in front of a house. The last rays of the dim afternoon sun glittered on the old termite-ridden wooden double door of the house. One of the doors was closed and the other was open. The corridor and the inside of the house were in total darkness. The girl could not make out what sort of a house it was or what was going on inside. She was exhausted, and her scratched leg burned. Her clothes were covered with dust; she resembled a traveler coming in from a long journey. She stood by the house, looked around her, and remembered the hustle and bustle of the bazaar and everything else which had attracted her attention or frightened her. She felt totally empty. The interesting part and the fear had both only been temporary. Here, finally, she screamed from the bottom of her heart and begged someone, anyone, to come to help her. But she was all alone; no one answered. She leaned her head helplessly against the old door. Four big nails stuck out of the wood, and an ugly knocker was nailed next to them. She took the knocker and beat it vigorously against the door. Suddenly, she thought of going into the house, but it was an unfamiliar place. She peeked through the half-open door; the house was dark. In those early hours of the evening, she could hear the noise of a single cricket coming from an unfamiliar tree in the yard. It seemed like the house was empty; nobody had answered, "Who is it?" The only noise she heard was the dry and muffled sound of the knocker echoing in the corridor. The little girl became frightened of the dark and the loneliness which enveloped her. She was totally exhausted, run down.

Hopelessly she began to cry. She sobbed loudly, hating being lost, but her voice did not reach anywhere. No one came to her rescue.

Her nanny was still looking for her in the bazaar, flirtatiously asking everyone after her, while the sound of the child's crying echoed in the dark corridor of the unfamiliar house like the dry muffled sound of the knocker.

The Accident

The trouble started from the time Sedigheh Khanoum,[2] our next-door neighbor, bought a car and took to the wheel wearing white gloves and a pair of dark glasses. I saw her as I walked out of the house that morning. She offered me a ride. Even though I didn't get in, I said my prayers in anticipation of what was to come, and it began that same afternoon at two o'clock. When I got home, my wife was in a foul mood. She answered my questions with a curt "yes" or "no." This was the wife who, every time I walked into the house, exclaimed, "Listen, I want to present my daily report. I'll speak my mind whether you want to listen or not. So keep your self-respect and listen." She would recount how every step she had taken had produced an

---

accident, and how Sedigheh Khanoum had done this or
that. But that day my wife was like a robot. She brought
in lunch which we ate in silence. For the first time she lit
a cigarette and clumsily put it to her lips and said, "Sit up
straight! I'd like to say something to you." I sat up straight.
My heart was in my mouth. She continued, "You have to
buy me a car, and you know that you will." I said, "Darling,
why are you speaking like the movie stars in dubbed films?"
"Don't act smart with me," she replied. "When will you
buy the car?" I said, "My dear, you don't even know how
to drive . . ."

"I found out all I needed to know from Sedigheh
Khanoum," she said. "Driving lessons, until I get my
license, will cost five hundred *tomans*. You can easily
borrow the money from your stingy office. Paying for the
car in installments is not to our benefit; if we can pay for
it in a lump sum, it will cost us only thirty-two thousand
tomans. A second-hand car is cheaper, of course, but it's
not worth it; it'll burn too much oil, and be in the repair
shop constantly. And you, God knows, never take a step
to help out your wife, so I'd be stuck having to plead with
the mechanics to fix it. They would probably cheat me
every time as well. No! Buy a new car."

True to form, she was the same old wife again. Actually,
I had always appreciated a talkative wife with a hearty
appetite and a healthy set of teeth. I had married Nadereh
for these very reasons. Of course, she was called Nadereh
when I first married her, but on the day of the wedding,
she insisted we change her name to Nadia.

I said, "Woman, you know full well that to earn
thirty-two thousand *tomans* is easier said than done. How

do you expect me to make that much money? You know my income can only cover our living expenses. We don't have a penny in savings. With two children in kindergarten and all the transportation expenses . . ."

It had slipped out, but what was done was done. My wife said triumphantly, "Yes, dear sir, and I want the car because of these transportation expenses. I'll drive you to the office in the morning and fetch you at noon. I'll take the children to the kindergarten. We'll be able to save a great deal."

"Woman, you've lost your mind," I said. "You're like someone who has no bread to eat, but makes room in the house for storing onions!"

She replied, "Well, he had the house; why didn't he mortgage it, dear? We, too, can mortgage our house. If in this whole world you only have a car, you have everything. You work in the savings and loan bank, don't you? You must be familiar with the procedure for these things."

I said, "Woman, all we own in the world is this house. You can't imagine how difficult it was for my father to put this house together. If we were to mortgage it, how would we earn the money to pay for the mortgage?"

She said, "Who knows? By then God will help." She swallowed and continued. "Look, darling, have I asked you for a palace or a trip to Europe? No. I didn't even have a proper wedding ceremony. My dream to wear a white gown with lace is still unfulfilled." She thought for a moment and then went on. "I recall once when I had a cold and asked you to buy me a fur coat; instead you suggested, 'Darling, why don't you take a Coricidin D?' " She pursed her lips. To keep her from crying, I said, "Let me rest for a while. I'll think about it later and see what can be done. Maybe I'll buy you a car on the installment plan." "No!" she exclaimed. "No installments. We are already slaves to consumption; we shall become slaves to installments as well." These were not her own words. They were even too much to be Sedigheh Khanoum's. Could it be that my wife was being unfaithful? God forbid! I should bite my tongue . . .

"What are you thinking about?" she asked. "Darling, you don't need to worry about the house. What kind of an area is Zargandeh anyway, with its gloomy sunsets? May God grant my father a long life, but not even he will live as long as Noah. The Bahman orchards will eventually become mine; then we'll buy a respectable house in Shemran. I've even thought about the area, either in Zaaferaniyeh or behind Bagheh Ferdows."

My wife was a gift from Ahwaz. In 1961,[3] for New Year's vacation, a few friends and I had gone to Ahwaz. We saw all there was to see in the city the first day, and we were left with nothing to do that night. We took a chance and decided to go to the movies. A whole group of schoolgirls was sitting in the row in front of us. They kept turning around and giggling, except for Nadereh (of the year 1961) or the present Nadia, who never turned around, not even once. We did not see the film; neither did the schoolgirls. After the national anthem and Pepsi and electric shaver commercials came the forthcoming attractions; then, suddenly, the film was stopped and the lights turned on. After a few minutes, the national anthem was

---

[3] 1961: 1340 in the Iranian calendar.

repeated and the advertisements started again. This cycle of stopping and starting was repeated three times. The third time, Nadereh stood up and shouted some slogans. "You're ridiculous. Nowhere in the world do they rerun the previews for every newcomer." Her voice resembled one of Radio Tehran's broadcasters. Perhaps she was trying to imitate her. Anyway, I shall not bore you, seeing the girls made us courageous. We, too, started to cheer and whistle. The theater became agitated, and we were all walked to the police station. In the station, she succeeded in charming both the officer in charge and me. It eventually became evident that the film had been restarted each time for the sake of some family member of the mayor, the governor general, or the chief of police, who had come late.

I told my wife, "It's better if you write to your dear father and ask him for an advance." She burst into a terrible sob. To calm her down, I told her, "Imagine you bought the car. Where, in this tiny house of ours without a garage, would you park it?" She dried her tears and exclaimed, "I knew you'd buy it! You're a good man, just too timid. I've thought about a space for the car. I'll buy a chain and tie the car at night to the concrete streetlight pole in front of our house. The first pole is for my car, the second is for Sedigheh Khanoum's."

It took three weeks for me to surrender. She would stand at the window facing the street, enviously staring at Sedigheh Khanoum's car and sighing. She refused to eat. I thought she was going to become ill.

I took a five hundred *toman* advance on my salary, and my wife took driving lessons. Then it was time to get her driver's license or, as she called it, her driving certificate. On orders from my mother, I purchased a copy of *Clues to Paradise*. I rummaged through the pages, hoping to find a prayer to render people stupid while practicing or to make people fail when taking their driver's exam. Of course, there was no such prayer in that book nor in any other prayer book. Mother went so far as to consult the Koran and vow that she would prepare a special ceremony and feed the poor if the devil that had invaded my wife's body, in the form of a car, would leave. Nevertheless, it eventually became obvious that this type of a devil could not be driven away no matter what magic was used—my wife passed the written test. She boasted later that she had answered every question correctly. The examining officer was so pleased that he complimented her: "Madame, you have stored up all of our southern sun," because my wife has a very dark complexion.[4]

She went on to say, "The officer asked me, 'If it has snowed and the road is icy and you brake while going downhill and the brakes fail, what would you do?' I replied, 'Honored examiner, I would not take my precious car out of the garage in such weather.' The officer placed his hands on his belly and had a hearty laugh." She also passed the Driving Skills test. She explained: "Akbar Agha,[5] the owner of the Volkswagen I took the test in, had dripped ink right on the curb. As I reached the ink drop, I turned

---

[4]Ahwaz, in the south of Iran, has a hot and sunny climate.

[5]Agha: mister or sir.

the wheel only a millimeter away from the curb line. I tipped him five *tomans*, later."

I started to have some hope in my mother's prayers, because my wife failed the 'stop the car between two poles' test three times. The first time, she had destroyed the poles altogether. The second time, she had succeeded in entering between the poles, but had failed to get out. The third time, she had had an argument with the officer. The officer was not, of course, the "southern sun" one; there were many officers in her tales. She had told the officer in charge of the 'stop the car between two poles' test, "Shorty, you have a complex because of your height and fail people without reason." She had acquired this type of knowledge by listening to Radio Tehran from dawn to dusk. The officer had therefore set her fourth test date two weeks later. I couldn't keep still from excitement, thinking that between pillar and post there might be hope. But then she passed the fourth test.

The traffic test was next. She failed six times. The first time, she forgot to put on her blinker before starting off. The second time, she forgot to look in the rear-view mirror. The third, she forgot to release the hand brake. The fourth, she had been tricked by the officer and stopped only a foot from the intersection. The fifth time, she had overtaken another car at high speed and in the wrong lane. The sixth time, no matter what she did, the car wouldn't start. The seventh time, it was probably a miracle that she had passed.

I mortgaged the house and borrowed thirty-five thousand *tomans*. To pay the installments every month, they would deduct five hundred *tomans* from my salary for ever and a day. "If in this whole world, you have a car, you have everything," my wife kept reminding me.

The first day she got up early, dressed, and slipped on her shoes. She wiped on purple lipstick, and put on a white scarf with purple spots, dark glasses and white gloves. I sat next to her, and the children sat in the back. She ordered them to stand up and watch, then she set off toward my office. She constantly mocked and teased the bus and taxi drivers and the pedestrians—especially the veiled women on the sidewalks. I started to get heartburn. By the time we had reached the office, my whole insides had twisted up and I had developed a monstrous stomach ache. I was fifteen minutes late, and an ulcer was threatening me.

She came to fetch me that afternoon. I had no choice but to get in. My heart began to pound.

At a red light on Istanbul Avenue, she put her left arm out the window to indicate she was turning. A thug grabbed her wrist and wouldn't let go. At first she dished out and got back some low-life slang, then she began to plead with him to let go of her hand. Finally she resorted to begging him. The thug, amazed at my wife, exclaimed, "Where on earth do you come from?" The traffic lights turned green, and we could go, but the creep wouldn't let go of her hand. My wife consoled me, saying "Remain calm, darling. These things happen when you drive." The cars behind us were honking away as if their drivers had to go reinvent the atom bomb. I was concerned for the watch on my wife's wrist; although it didn't work, it was gold. I was reluctant to get out of the car and tackle the thug because cars were passing by us at the speed of light, and I'm the type of person who's even scared of parked cars lest they suddenly start to move.

She considered it her duty to drive me to and from work every day, and it was impossible to relieve her of this sense of responsibility. Danger threatened my entire being. My pride constantly incited me to defend her, but I either restrained these dutiful feelings or simply ignored the situation altogether. But most of all I was short of cash.

I knocked on every door in the office until I finally got an out-of-town assignment to the Mishan desert.

Her letters were filled with tales of driving escapades. I have them all in front of me. "Darling, yesterday I went to Naderi Avenue to pick up my clothes; I had them dyed. I know I shall not see new clothes for some time now. Because of late payment on the loan last month, they have taken forty-five *tomans* and three *rials* out of your salary. To hell with the bloody misers. Well, anyway, I was telling you about going to Naderi Avenue. I parked the car by the embassy. There wasn't a car either in front or behind me. My clothes were not ready, so I thought I'd go and browse around the stores in the shopping arcade. You should have seen the shirts on sale! Bandannas are in fashion now as well; a bandanna is a half-circle made of cloth and cotton and is perfect for drivers. They put it around their head so their hair doesn't get messed up.

"I got my dresses and returned to the car. A long Cadillac was parked in front of my car and a dilapidated Volkswagen behind it. I said to myself, 'The hell with it,' and got behind the wheel. I don't know what I did to get my right front bumper hooked on the Cadillac's back bumper and my back bumper locked into the Volkswagen's front bumper. There was no way for me to move the car, so I got out. The schools had just let out, and the area was swarming with big high school jocks. As they passed, every one of them sent a snickering smart-ass remark my way. One of them went so far as to say, 'Lady Delkash,[6] sing us a song?'

"I stopped a decent looking man, who stepped out of his car and came to my rescue. He admitted it was a bad bumper-to-bumper lock. He called on two carwash boys with their long multicolored checkered rags on their shoulders, who in turn got hold of two laborers. Together they lifted the Volkswagen off the ground and put it down a good distance from my Peugeot. I don't know what happened, but I backed up too far and hit the Volkswagen. It's not a car, it's cardboard. I had crumpled it. Of course, I took out my card, wrote down my address, and left it on the Volkswagen's windshield. I hope to God the owner doesn't come after me."

"Darling," her next letter began, "no sign of the Volkswagen owner. Sedigheh Khanoum says he probably didn't believe I'd left the right address; no fool would have. The day before yesterday, I got myself into trouble again. Fortunately, I wriggled out of it unharmed. Passing through the Abass Abad district, I noticed that all oncoming cars were flashing their lights at me. I thought they were saying hello, so I replied by turning on my windshield wipers. You know what? The road ahead was closed; I found out at the intersection. You can't imagine the difficulty I had in turning around. Of course not—you don't even know how to drive! I took the turn too wide and hit a Volkswagen which was parked for no reason in the

---

[6]Delkash was a renowned Persian woman singer. Delkash also literally means heartthrob.

middle of the road. You know what? Its engine had stalled, and my hitting it started it up again. But I wasn't to know that! I was having a fit about how I would get the money to pay for the damages. At the Ghasr intersection, the lights turned red. I gasped, 'My Lord, he's going to catch up with me and ask for damages.' Instead the man thanked me. It was only then that I realized what had happened. In my usual polite fashion, I said, 'My pleasure. We drivers ought to help one another.' He'll find out the damage I've done when he reaches his destination, but 'tomorrow is too late.' "

"By the way, darling, I was forced to instigate a little coup d'etat at home. I sold the glass top table, whose glass always broke, and that easy chair of yours and the dilapidated foyer rug for 360 *tomans*. You know, one day I forgot to release the hand brake and drove all the way to Varamin with the brakes on. I was going to visit your dear aunt. I wasn't doing it for your sake; I went because I wanted to practice my driving and improve my sense of direction. The brake linings and wheel bearings were burned up and cost me 360 *tomans* to fix."

My assignment was over, and I returned to Tehran. I knew I would find the house empty like a mosque. My wife's coup d'etats were dangerous and she also lacked any sense of direction. I had worked a great deal to help her acquire

a proper sense of direction. When she first started to drive
I had slipped out a map of Tehran for her from the office.
But she couldn't make sense of it. Then I realized that she
knew nothing about the points of the compass. I tried to
teach her at least where north was by using the sun and its
movement. I had her stand facing north with open arms,
teaching her as we had learned in the sixth grade. I told
her, "Now your right arm is pointing to the east and your
left arm to the west. Facing you is the north and behind
you is the south." She said, "But, darling, there is no sun
at night, and besides, what am I going to do on a cloudy
day?" I resolved the night problem with the help of the Big
Dipper. Unfortunately, she could not make heads or tails
of either the Big or the Little Dipper. I explained to her
that because the Kaaba[7] is in the south, mosques are built
north to south, facing the Kaaba. But my wife had never
prayed in her life. I explained that the church gates always
faced east, but churches were not on every street. Finally,
I tried to arouse her curiosity. I cannot remember where I
had read, or perhaps heard, that ants build their mounds
facing north. Perhaps I made it up myself. She liked this
one a lot, but not for the sake of her driving, just for fun.
Everywhere we went she found the ant trails, followed
them and said, "They're going toward the north because
their homes are built facing north." I bought her a Razmara
compass, but she fiddled with it so much it stopped working.

---

[7]Kaaba: a small shrine located near the center of the Great Mosque in Mecca and
considered by Muslims everywhere to be the most sacred spot on earth. Muslims
orient themselves toward this shrine during the five daily prayers, bury their dead
facing its meridian, and cherish the ambition of visiting it on pilgrimage, in accord
with the command of God in the Koran.

I got home. My wife and the children had lost so much weight they looked like spiders and spindles. My wife's explanations about the car's problems were so technical that they were way beyond me. For example: the ball bearing was stuck in the stubaxle, or vice-versa. The distributor cable was torn, and the generator refused to produce sparks; or the clutch disc was warped, and so on and so forth. My wife would drive the children to kindergarten and return home, change into a pair of pants—American style. She would fill her recently purchased red plastic pail with water, add some washing powder to it, and wearing her plastic gloves, attack the car, washing it as if there were no tomorrow. She sang, too. Her expertise exceeded that of the carwash boys. She would clean the car so well that you could see your reflection in it. She had also bought a radio for the car from the sale of the ventilator fan, saying, "Why did we need a ventilator fan in the middle of winter? And summer is so far away."

I really told her off. I even felt like beating her up. But seeing her so thin, her eyes hollowed out and racing around, standing there in one of her dyed dresses, I felt sorry for her.

Once again, I thought of finding myself another assignment. I exerted so much effort in search of one that I finally collapsed and was bed-ridden; perhaps it was from sorrow. My wife took truly excellent care of me. Mother, as well, would come every day, all the way from Paghapogh, to cook me soup. My wife would drive her back at night. When she returned, she would describe, playing with the car keys, which roads she had chosen, which cars she had overtaken, and how much verbal abuse she had heard. One night she was late, and I began to worry. At nine o'clock the phone rang; my wife's voice on the line sounded so terrified that I truly felt sorry "Darling, don't be afraid, nothing's happened. I've only had an accident," she said.

"An accident?"

"Yes."

"With whom?"

"With a traffic officer."

"A traffic officer?" My God! Life turned dark before my eyes. Of all the people in the world! She had had an accident with a traffic officer. How could anyone challenge their word?

"Not with him, with his motorcycle. Collect whatever money there is in the house, with my license—my license is in the sewing machine box—and bring them over to the police station, the Tupkhaneh police station. The man is talking about three thousand *tomans*."

I dressed up like a go-getter; red tie, suede jacket, slanted hat, and walked into the station. My temperature must have been 102, but my wife later told me, "Your entrance was wonderful, darling." I said, "Gentlemen, what has my wife done? Has she committed first degree murder?"

My wife, sitting on a bench in a corner, appeared so frightened and miserable that my heart went out to her. Seeing me, she was encouraged and stood up, saying "I swear to God it wasn't my fault at all. The policeman's recorded it in his report. I dropped off your mother, and on the way back the traffic had come to a standstill in front of the Ministry of Health. Why? Because Mr. Brezhnev and his entourage were visiting the Red Cross. This Mister

Warrant Officer (I looked at the man's badge; he was a captain) was part of Mr. Brezhnev's escort and was supposed to be following the group. Why should he have parked his oversized motorcycle in the middle of the street? When we could move again, a pickup truck turned in front of me, and I had to pull out to avoid him. It was then that I hit the motorcycle. If only you knew what the crowds did to me. They almost tore me apart. Those bloody sycophants who'd been herded to cheer Mr. Brezhnev kept yelling and calling me 'Lady Delkash.' 'Lady Delkash' was the least of their insults. They said such awful things to me." Then she burst into tears.

The captain said, "The only thing we have in the world is our motorcycle, and the streets really belong to us . . . We'll park wherever we like. The lady was driving without a license. Her fine is . . ."

I interrupted him and took my wife's license from my pocket and held it in front of his eyes. He snatched the license and I was too scared to take him on. Actually, I'm scared of both traffic and traffic officers. What can I do? It's not my fault.

My wife quipped, "Bravo for your manhood! You gave away the license which I had earned with my sweat and blood." And she began to cry again.

Another captain came forward with the police report. He said "Come on now, make peace. You, sir, replace whatever's been broken or shattered on the captain's motorcycle, and captain, return the lady's license."

We agreed. My wife sat behind the wheel, with shaky hands, and I sat next to her. The captain sat in the back. We searched every single parts shop along Cheragh Bargh

Avenue until we found a new windshield for the
motorcycle, along with a new front light and bracket. All
the time my wife kept advising the captain to be less
concerned with the beauty and appearance of his vehicle.
She said, "The important thing is what's in one's head, by
way of brains and intelligence. What's the use of being so
spruced up?" She went on. "The characteristics of
underdeveloped nations are that their captains are covered
with glitter and gold, and their women only care for their
appearance. In these countries, the number of shoe shines,
taxis, hairdressers, and liquor stores far exceed the number
of bookstores." It was all a nice lullaby, but the words were
not my wife's. Could it be that my wife . . .

We couldn't find the motorcycle's factory emblem, and
our search was postponed until the next day. The next
morning, my fever was gone; together with my wife and
the captain we searched every single junk shop on Amir
Kabir Avenue. The emblem wasn't to be found. The
captain threatened to keep my wife's license until we found
the emblem. My wife swore that she would go and see the
brigadier general saying, "According to the policeman's
report, you were supposed to be following Mr. Brezhnev."
The captain went pale and immediately returned her
license. We had already spent two hundred *tomans*. Had
she made the threat earlier and actually gone to the
brigadier general in the first place, we wouldn't have wasted
the two hundred *tomans*.

I looked until I found another assignment. This time, I
went to Bandar Shah. My wife's letters were short and
unenlightening. She neither wrote about the car nor
mentioned any new coup d'etats in the house. Slowly, I

came to believe that she had forsaken the love of the car and
that our lives would fall into the old routine. I wrote her a
few hearty letters. I wrote about the night in the police
station at Ahwaz and how she had me fall in love with her
overnight. I wrote about the next day when we were taking
a stroll along the boulevard next to the railroad tracks and
my wife was saying, "My favorite color is blue and my
favorite book is *In the Shade of the Sisphon Trees*," and that
later her favorite book had become *The Book of Feathers*. I
reminded her of the day of our wedding when she had
worn a blue dress and had said the "yes" in a rush, without
allowing the mullah to read the marriage sermon three times
before she said "yes," as is customary. Slowly, in my
letters, I came to think of having a third baby. I went even
further and proposed that we sell the car, explaining how
we could save on a few installment payments. My wife
suddenly took to silence. I sent her a response-required
telegram. The reply came. "We're fine, Nadia." And,
again, silence.

I took a leave of absence and came back to Tehran. At
the Zarab Khaneh intersection, a badly destroyed car had
been put up for display. The car was completely mutilated,
but I recognized it. It was my wife's Peugeot. My wife was
probably dead by now; no one after an accident like that
could have a single unscathed spot left on his body. I asked
the cab driver how long the Peugeot had been on display.
He replied, "About a month." I asked, "Do you know
what happened to the driver?" He did not know. By the
time I reached home, I was half dead. My wife opened the
door. She was dressed in black from head to toe, with black
lace over her hair. I asked, "Who's dead? Mother? The

children?" She said, "Don't worry, no one is dead."

"Then why are you wearing black?"

"I had a bad accident. I was coming from a side street onto the main road and I hit a colonel." Her voice was her own; she wasn't imitating anyone, not the radio broadcasters nor the actresses of dubbed movies.

"But I still don't understand why you're wearing mourning clothes then," I said.

"It's been a month since the colonel entered the hospital," she said. "The poor man is bandaged from head to foot. I go to the Army Hospital every day to visit him and hopefully convince him not to sue us. I came back from the hospital only a minute ago. I've told the colonel that I'm a widow and my husband died recently, and I'm wearing black so maybe he'll feel sorry for me. Otherwise, God knows, we'll have to pay thousands in damages."

We went into the room and I asked her, "Where are the children?"

"They're with Sedigheh Khanoum," she said, and she was telling the truth; she went and fetched them. The next morning, she put on her black clothes and lace again. After dressing up the poor kids in black as well, she took them to the Army Hospital to visit the colonel. She had taught them to start crying and wailing as soon as they saw the colonel, but to absolutely not say a word.

My leave was coming to an end and, according to my wife, the colonel was recovering. They had now uncovered both his eyes, and he had been able to walk to the bathroom on his own. My wife was extremely happy.

It was my last night home. I was about to bring up the issue of the third baby when my wife suddenly lit up and

said, "Sit up straight. I want to tell you about a problem."
My heart failed. I truly could not buy another car.

She continued, "You know dear? I'm against the preser-
vation of marriage. Marriage is an act of the bourgeoisie."

These words were not my wife's. They were definitely
not Sedigheh Khanoum's, and they couldn't be the colonel's
either. These were the words of a person who knew about
consumption, installments, underdeveloped nations, taxis,
shoe-shiners, officer's glitter and gold . . . and women.
I took a chance and asked her, "Are you planning to divorce
me?"

She smiled and said, "Yes, you've got it right. You know
full well that you'll give me a divorce, so keep your
self-respect and start working out the details."

I continued, "You plan to marry a man who has spoken
of the bourgeoisie . . ."

She said, "No, he's not into marriage and that sort of
thing."

"Have you known him for long?" I asked. My blood was
boiling.

"No," she said, "I've only seen him a few times at
Sedigheh Khanoum's house."

"Then why do you want a divorce?" I asked. "It's ok
with me, but the children will be miserable."

"That's my affair," she said.

We had a fight over dinner, and I beat her up while the
children cried hysterically. I returned to Bandar Shah, but
she persistently wrote so many letters asking for her
divorce, that I finally gave up my assignment, returned to
Tehran, and granted her wish.

Three months and eleven days later, my wife, wearing

a white gown with lace, was married to the colonel. The children were sent to Mother, and I remained alone, numbed and saddled with the installment payments to the savings and loan. And the colonel did not sue for damages.

Clay female figurine with raised hairstyle and gold earring
Iran, Amlash; 9th century B.C.

The Playhouse

Mehdi Siah looked in the mirror. He took the red cape off the nail and draped it over his clothes, saying: "Now we're ready. But alas! Where is your whip, eunuch of the Caliph's court?" He found the whip on the nail from which hung the Caliph's robe. He took it. Mehdi Siah always came earlier than the other actors because blacking[8] his face, hands, and neck took a long time. What's more, washing off the black was even harder than putting it on; he therefore also always had to leave later than everyone else.

The small door connecting the playhouse auditorium to the area backstage, which was a lengthy corridor with all

---

[8]In traditional Persian theatre, blacking the face is a disguise that enables the actor to do and say things which would otherwise be unacceptable, in the same way the fool is often used by Shakespeare. Siah also means black in Persian.

the typical characteristics, was opened. A short, young man with curly hair bent his head and walked in. Siah stood facing him. He asked: "Who the hell are you? Look, brother, no one is allowed in the playhouse." He turned on a switch, and a bright light lit the theater. He looked at the short man and continued. "What kind of creature are you? Oh, God! I think I'm going to be scared. Look at his ring; it's got a skull on it. See his tie pin; it's a diamond. What kind of oats are you looking for, all dressed up in this stable? Where do you think you're going with all your glitz?" He laughed and laughed and raised his whip. The young man asked: "Are you the famous Mehdi Siah?"

"Mehdi Siah, I am, but I didn't know I was famous."

"I've heard people come to this theater only to see you."

"Yeah, brother," said Siah. "People laugh because of me at night, and at me in the morning."

The young man introduced himself.

"I've come to replace Mohsen. He's sick. He said I had to become Juji Khan. But I don't know how. I'm scared. I've never been on stage before."

Siah wanted to laugh and tease the young novice. Whatever he was, famous or unknown, being witty was Siah's specialty. When he disappeared into his adopted skin, a witty personality would awaken in him. But when he was himself, one could no longer say he even had a personality. He saw himself as a total stranger in the world. On stage, people's eyes were fixed on him alone. But off stage, there were no eyes on him at all. He was tempted to tease the young man. Usually he never missed these opportunities to exercise his wit. But helping people was also one of his unfailing specialties. He said: "Don't be scared, nobody knows which role they'll be playing."

"Don't you read the play first? Don't you rehearse?"

"No, brother," said Siah. "None of that stuff here. The opening night of each play, the owner of the playhouse comes, tells the story, and decides each person's role. Then we wear our costumes and go off to act. The first night is difficult for everyone; afterwards it becomes routine. The important thing is for the first person to start off well."

"You mean you improvise? Well, that's quite difficult. Even if I had rehearsed beforehand I'd still be scared to go on the stage."

Siah was about to say: "Impro . . . what? Watch out you don't get struck by the evil eye!" But he didn't. Instead he tried to encourage the young man and said: "This is no sophisticated playhouse in Petelbourg. It's a dilapidated theater next to the fruit and vegetable market. Who do you suppose the audience is? A bunch of experts? Full of themselves with thick cigars in their mouths? People who don't even smile when everyone else is falling over with laughter? No, my friend. Here we deal with fruit and vegetable vendors, porters, drivers, and gravediggers. After they have delivered their loads or buried their dead, they come to seek us. Entertaining this kind of crowd is not such a difficult task."

Siah helped the young man get dressed. He had him wear a tight robe and tied a scarf around it. Using a piece of coal, he raised his eyebrows and fixed the corners of his eyes to match. "Go on, look at yourself in the mirror," said Siah. "Now, you are Juji Khan, the son of the King of China, who has to ask for the Caliph's daughter's hand in marriage. And me, I am the castle guard."

Juji Khan went toward the mirror in which Siah was observing him. He said: "Thanks a lot. What are these shabby clothes! Besides, this costume is not even Chinese."

Siah was offended. Not because he wanted to defend the theater, no. He was defending his own beliefs. "Brother, what you say is both right and wrong. I have made your face Chinese, that should be enough. You have to act well so that the audience understands from your face and acting that you are Chinese. Besides, is my costume a black's? Is the Caliph's costume a real Caliph's? Look, these clothes hanging from the nails are all that this theater owns in the world. That torn one over there is the costume of the Caliph of Baghdad. And that is his tuft. The other one there is the civil servant's costume. That one is the witch's costume. That one belongs to the lover, and the other is the Haji's costume. These costumes are needed in every play. There's always a lover who foolishly falls in love with the King's daughter and there appear rivals who come from everywhere. And eventually he either wins the girl or loses her. And I'm the guard, in other words, Haji's servant. But I feel sorry for the lovers. Secretly, I help them. And let me tell you this, too; the girl's really worth falling in love with. You'll see, as soon as you set eyes on her, your acting will naturally improve."

They became silent. They sat facing each other on the empty benches backstage. From where he was sitting Mehdi Siah could see himself in the mirror. The room was cold, and Mehdi had put his hands under his arms. He was not wearing his red hat yet, and his eyes were searching for it. When he saw the hat had fallen on a bench, he was relieved.

The young man's words, "People come to this theater for you," had put him in a thoughtful mood. He had confidence in his own talent. Most of his colleagues had a drink to overcome their fear before going on the stage. He, however, needed neither drink nor any other kind of stimulant. For him to become "black" was the most natural act. When he appeared, he brilliantly mastered both stage and audience. His concentration was amazingly intense. Novices had their eyes fixed on his lips, and at times they would forget where they were. It was he who had to coax them to remember their lines. He did all the work, but others got to make love to the girl. When it came time to witness the love-making, a deep sorrow would engulf his heart, until the audience snapped him out of it: "Siah, dear, don't doze off!" If ever he was a moment late on stage the entire audience would whistle and call for him. And he would smoothly and comfortably continue his part. Despite all this, Siah had never heard a word of admiration from the owner of the playhouse nor from any of his colleagues. And the admiration of the audience was confined to those few hours of the play; next morning no one even recognized him.

The young man watched Siah with interest. "Where did you learn how to act?" he asked. "Did you study acting?"

"No. I haven't had much of an education, but I've seen quite a bit of blackness and intrigue in my life. Besides, I only know how to play the role of the 'black Siah.' "

"I always thought, with all your mastery, you must have studied for years," said the young man.

"In my forty-odd years, there hasn't been a trick I haven't played, from storytelling to narrating epics of the *Shahnameh* in the coffee house. For a long time I was a storyteller and poetry reader to the grand nephew of Zell-ol Sultan. I've also fooled around with political parties. And for twenty years now, I have played the role of 'Siah' in the theater. Don't you think that's enough? There are times when one asks oneself: Is it I who's done all this living? Is it I who's witnessed all these tricks?"

The young man stood up. He wanted to say something but was too shy. He stood in front of the mirror, his back to Siah, and muttered:

"I wanted to say that . . . I am a graduate of the School of Acting. But I don't have one bit of your courage. I'm even scared to step up on the stage. Very scared."

"Then what have they taught you in school? Eh?" asked Siah.

The young man turned around. He sat next to Siah and said: "They taught us plenty in school, but there were also many things they didn't teach us, many things. And maybe it's me who's timid. Once I was supposed to play Hamlet. I had rehearsed quite a bit, but as I was about to step onto the stage, I secretly peeked at the auditorium. I saw that, besides my classmates, a few strangers had also come. I got the butterflies. I didn't go on stage at all."

Siah's wit broke out. "You said H'omelet? Well, it obviously wasn't your fault at all. We don't go much for making omelets; ours is an eggplant dish, 'Kashk-e Bademjan.'"

The young man laughed and said:

"Even though you've never studied acting, nevertheless, because of your tremendous experiences, you have an extensive knowledge of culture. Your talent is also extraordinary. And even more important, I don't know why, but one feels like confiding in you." Then he continued: "Do you know what the greatest tragedy is?"

"Listen brother, if you want to talk like a foreigner," replied Siah, "you and I won't get along. Can't you talk normal?"

"To tell the truth," said the young man, "I can speak any way you like. I speak quite well. It's only when I have to appear on stage that I become speechless. I have so many words in my head, but I can't utter them at the right moment. Once, in school, we were supposed to present the play *Our Beloved Country, Iran*. I was holding a box of matches in my hand. My role was to go and light the lantern on stage and say: 'O light of guidance, route of flight for the Iranian people, remain alight.' It was only one sentence. That night a few army officers were wandering about backstage. One of them came up to me and asked: 'What do you plan to do with those matches?' I became dumb. The officer searched my pockets. Do you think I could go on stage that night? No way! I had the butterflies again."

"Here again, it wasn't your fault," said Mehdi Siah sympathetically. "You were going to speak of the greatest foreign imitation of all."

"The greatest of tragedies."

"I, too, have heard of these things," Siah was about to say, but he changed his mind and waited.

"Excuse me," said the young man. "I was talking about the saddest of things. I believe the saddest thing in the world is when someone aspires to become a first-rate actor, painter, or poet but, despite his efforts, he fails. Sometimes it may be because he has to start earning a living; that is different. But the person who sacrifices everything and still can't—that's tragedy."

"You are right," said Siah. "You do speak well. I'm surprised you say you can't act. Then why did you substitute for Mohsen tonight?"

"I want to test myself one more time. Mohsen told me that you help motivate all the actors, without even being aware of it yourself. I thought if one gets to know a man who may give one a push—just a little push—maybe one will get going. Some go on their own. Some go without even knowing it. Others are untalented, but get ahead with a lot of noise and clamor and cunning and cheating. But there are those who can't go alone. If one is lucky enough to meet a real man . . ."

"What about a real woman?" asked Siah with a wink.

"You mean if one falls in love . . .?" began the young man.

His words were interrupted. The other actors, bending their heads as they walked through the low door, came backstage. The room became crowded. The Caliph was gluing on his beard. The lover was putting on his make-up. The witch was disheveling her hair. The manager was explaining Juji Khan's role to him, and Siah heard the young man mention "Acting School," but nothing of his fear. The actors went and sat down one by one. The Caliph lit his cigarette and told Siah, "Brother, check out the auditorium; see if it is full yet."

Siah slowly went toward the small door, dragging his feet behind him. He heard his colleagues' laughter. He peeked in through the crack of the door and saw a street sweeper in his municipal uniform sitting in the front row, right across from the curtain, cracking pumpkin seeds between his teeth. Siah liked his air, especially as he was sitting in the front stalls. "Great," he whispered, then returned and told the Caliph:

"There are a few here and there."

Toward the end of the first act, right in the middle of things, the power went out. The stage and auditorium fell into a grave-like darkness. There was a moment of silence, and then chatter and clamor rose from the crowd. The street sweeper flicked his lighter and stood up, holding it in front of the stage. Some of the others lit matches. The children in the audience were scared and cried. The noise of chairs clattering was heard from the back of the auditorium. "Whoever has hidden anything, eat it now! Fast!" said Siah out loud. Only a few people laughed, which upset him. He said louder: "Are you having a nightmare?" This time nobody was listening to him to laugh. Siah changed his mind about entertaining the giant crowd which had begun to move. He saw the Caliph's daughter in the dark as she walked in through the castle door. She came close to Siah and whispered in his ear: "Siah, dear, I'm going to be ill." The audience was whistling loudly and clapping hard. Darkness as black as tar had spread every-where. The street sweeper's lighter had gone out. Siah took a look at the crowd. He imagined a thousand-handed monster clinging on to various spots with each hand.

"What are you waiting for? Take me away, otherwise I'll faint right here."

Siah took the Caliph's daughter's hand. It was wet.

Fumbling in the dark they left the stage and climbed up the stairs to the backstage area. As he opened the ladies' changing room door, the women, the two nurses of the Caliph's daughter, let out screams. "Calm down," said Siah. "Siah's not bothering anyone. The Caliph's daughter's ill."

He took the girl toward the only bench in the room and had her lie down. He told one of the nurses: "Sister, will you get a glass of water?" The nurse left the room. "I hope she'll find a lamp and bring it back with her," said Siah. He turned toward the other nurse and said; "Come and open her dress."

The monstrous-looking nurse moved round the room, bent over the girl's chest, fiddled a bit and said:

"The knot's tangled. I can't untie it. Agha Mehdi, come and see; perhaps you can undo it."

Perhaps Siah could and wanted to, but it didn't happen. The nurse tore open the decorative filigree crisscrossing the girl's breasts. Siah could hear her as she asked the Caliph's daughter:

"Has he quarreled with you again?"

"Yes."

"He left?"

"Of course."

"I said from the very beginning that he is crazy. He spends well, but still, he's crazy. You poor woman, you'd better think about yourself now. Am I not right, Agha Mehdi?"

Siah, who was standing perplexed in the middle of the room, came beside the girl's bed. He sat on the bare floor and said in a fatherly fashion, "What can I say? All I know is that you are badly wrecking your life, girl. Don't you think it's a pity?"

He wished he could sit there forever next to the girl's bed, on the bare floor in the dark. He wished he could untie the tangled knot in the girl's life. He noticed the nurse in the dark who came and sat beside the bed and asked: "Did you take the pills?"

"I took them all right," the girl said, "but what's the use? These pills only make me ill. They don't get rid of *it*, and give me peace!"

The other nurse walked in with a lit candle and a bowl of water. She gave the candle to Mehdi, who, seeing her, had stood up. Her black eyes gleamed for a moment in the candlelight. "The show is over," she said. "There's no electricity. The crowd broke a few chairs. Two of them were arrested and taken to the station by the police. We'll see no money tonight."

Siah put the candle on the shelf above the Caliph's daughter's head. He was thinking that only Juji Khan could be happy about the show's closing. Juji Khan was to come on stage in the second act. Involuntarily he thought about the litter he had suggested they build for Juji Khan so that he would not panic as he came on stage. They had inserted wooden poles in the four sides of a handbarrow. A printed cloth hanging all around served as a curtain; Juji Khan was supposed to sit inside. The previous nights, Juji Khan had entered the stage on foot along with his four ministers and courtiers.

Siah looked at the Caliph's daughter, who was sitting up and asking the nurse: "Are they really not going to pay us tonight?"

"I don't suppose so," said the nurse. "The officer said
we have to return the audience's money."

"Then lend me twenty *tomans*."

"I swear I haven't got any."

The Caliph's daughter lowered her head and murmured:
"I have to take at least ten more of these pills, and each pill
costs two *tomans*."

Siah thrust his hand under his red cape and searched his
vest pockets. He took out a few bills. The Caliph's daughter
embraced him and stuck her face to his, saying: "How good
you are, Siah." Siah felt his neck become wet. When the
Caliph's daughter lifted her head, Siah knew that her face
too, must have become black.

The following night at the new Juji Khan's insistence, Mehdi
had a drink. He never drank before the show. The show itself naturally warmed him up. It was only after the show
that sorrow, indolence, and fatigue would overtake him.
Mehdi blackened himself carefully. He wet his hand and
straightened the crease in the red cape. The cape was old
and torn in places; it smelled damp. Struggling with witches
and the girl's lovers was no easy task. Juji Khan had dressed
by himself and was preparing the litter. But his face was
pale, and Siah knew he was frightened. The Caliph, the ministers, the witch, the lover, and the civil servants were all
ready; Siah had let them know that the theater was packed
and that a few foreigners were sitting in the front row. One
of them even had a camera with him. The street sweeper
was sitting in exactly the same place as the night before.

The third bell rang, and the show began. Siah took his whip and joyfully entered the Caliph's palace. He appeared on the palace terrace, and the audience laughed when they saw him. He cast an indifferent look at the crowd, sunk in darkness. The lover entered the stage. He stood in front of the side door of the palace. He began to wail and confess to a moon, which was supposed to be in the stage sky, but was not. He pretended to be counting the stars. Siah was waiting for the Caliph's daughter to come and chase him away from the palace terrace so that she could make secret plans with her lover. She was late, but Siah was confident that she would show up. Waiting for the girl, he walked through the cardboard door which led to the stage a few times, threatening the lover with his whip. The audience laughed. He knew that once he went to the palace, he would see the girl. He almost rushed there, but the girl was nowhere to be seen. The lover's confessions to the moon, his counting of the stars, and Siah's threats were repeated a few times. Siah sensed the crowd's irritation. The fourth time he went into the palace and saw the playhouse manager, looking very upset, standing next to the door. "The girl hasn't shown up," he whispered to Siah. "I don't know what to do!"

Keeping an ear on the lover's confessions, Siah asked: "She hasn't shown up? How could she do this to us? This poor guy has run out of things to confess."

"How about sending one of the nurses?" said the manager.

"How could we—they are old hags."

"Then do me a favor; keep the audience entertained; perhaps she'll show up."

Siah came onto the stage with his whip. The lover, dumbfounded, stared at the palace terrace. Siah went close to him and facing the audience said: "Don't wait for her in vain. The Caliph's daughter is not coming; your lover . . ." He was about to say "is dead," but unintentionally said: "is pregnant." The audience broke out in laughter. Siah was encouraged and continued; "That's right, brother, she's pregnant. Why are you dumfounded? Can't the Caliph's daughter become pregnant? Why do you look so lost?"

And, indeed, the lover appeared completely lost. He stared at Siah in astonishment. He asked silently: "Have you lost your mind?"

But a spectator in the front row shouted, "Siah, are you sure it wasn't your doing?"

Siah didn't like that. He rolled his eyes in anger and said: "Hey you, toughs, thugs, dandies, foreigners, photographers, veiled ones . . ." He was about to say ". . . unveiled ones," but he said "vile ones" and the audience laughed but not very hard. "No, don't laugh. Let me tell you the truth. Hey you, sitting there in the dark, with eyes gleaming like a cat's. Don't think I am joking around. Do you see this Siah? He's not one who takes liberties with others' loved ones. His eyes and heart are pure, and his word is the word of justice. The Caliph's daughter who is not here yet is not one of those either . . ." The sound of one person's laughter was heard from the back of the auditorium. This laughter among the silence of the audience was painful for Siah. He corrected himself: "No, brother. The Caliph's daughter is not one of those girls, she is just like your Siah. We are all like Siahs. One or two among us are not, though . . ."

Siah felt a commotion among the crowd, from irritation.

He was constantly sensitive to every one of the crowd's reactions. "Allow me to dance," he continued. "Have you come to watch a wailing ritual? Then clap your hands. What are you waiting for? Siah dances. He should be dancing . . ." As he danced, Siah came across the lover who was standing stupefied in the middle of the stage. He said: "Why are you watching me so dumfounded?" "I don't get it," said the lover slowly, so that only Siah could hear. Ignoring the lover's confusion, Siah asked: "Tell me, brother, which is worse; being in love or being hungry?"

The lover did not answer. A man's voice rose from the audience: "If you've ever had to relieve yourself and not found a place, you'll know it's worse than both." The people laughed and a couple clapped. But Siah didn't like it. He turned and distanced himself from the lover. He wheeled around, faced the crowd, and said with a sad voice, "Siah danced and while he danced he came across the Caliph's daughter, who's pregnant, who's been forsaken by her husband. Now the Caliph's daughter has gone to the blacksmiths' row to order an iron outfit—iron shoes, iron socks, an iron cane, and an iron ring. When they're ready she'll wear them and set out for the desert, searching for her husband." There was a lump in Siah's throat. "I shouldn't have had that drink," he thought to himself. He tried to get control of himself. He couldn't. He started to clap and said: "Laugh, clap, have fun. This is Juji Khan's theatre. But what's Juji Khan's problem? Juji Khan doesn't know that there is a treasure hidden in the hearts of human beings. Sometimes there is also a green viper sleeping on top of this untouched treasure. You have to say a prayer and blow it toward the snake. God willing it will become your captive. Then at your own leisure you can go to the treasure and take as much as you please. There is no end to it. Close your eyes and suddenly leap in the water. Don't be afraid. What are you afraid of? The treasure in your heart won't allow you to drown. It will force you to swim. You'll eventually get somewhere. In the depths of the hearts of every one of us lies a treasure. We only have to somehow crush the head of the snake, whose name is fear. Perhaps we can cast a spell upon it. But what if the snake is not sleeping on top of the treasure inside one's heart, but is sitting and waiting on the outside? What if, no matter how honestly, one uses this God-entrusted treasure, but nevertheless is always defeated, always stopped, just like hitting a wall head on, flattening one's nose? What if no spell could charm the snake sitting on the outside?"

The street sweeper sitting in the front row sneezed loudly. Siah took notice and thought: "He sneezed on purpose to warn me." Facing the janitor, he said: "Bless you, brother." Over in the corner, he caught sight of the two policemen in the auditorium. They were there every night, and he knew it. But tonight he really felt their presence. "Siah dances," he said. "While dancing he comes across the cop. The cop thinks I'm a beggar. He imagines I'm a crook. He sees my matchbox in my hand. He supposes that I plan to set fire to the Gheisarieh district. He asks what I intend to do with the matches. Brother, with these matches I want to light the fairy's strand of hair so that she may appear before your very eyes. Or shall I light Seemorgh the phoenix's feather so that it may come to your aid? Isn't it a wonderful idea, officer?"

The audience's clamor brought the lover out of his

helpless state and stopped Siah from continuing with what he was about to say. The lover took a step and said: "Ah, my love, I shall perish in anticipation." And he ran toward the terrace.

Siah turned and looked. He saw one of the nurses dressed up in the Caliph's daughter's clothes. The dress looked horrible on her body. Her dentures, her frizzed hair, and her frightened eyes made Siah sick. He felt no compassion. "She's a fake, she's a fake," he yelled. "Nobody's love will come. Nobody's love will ever come."

The fake Caliph's daughter, the old woman standing in the terrace, said: "Shut up. I will have His Majesty the Caliph cut off your head and fill your straw with skin and hang you from the palace wall. Hang . . ." The fake Caliph's daughter could not pronounce the word correctly.

"Sister, now see what you've done," Siah said out loud. "Does a wise man fill the straw with skin, or the skin with straw?"

"My love, the one who has no rival in Baghdad," said the lover, "I implore you to pardon the Siah for my sake."

"She'd wish!" said Siah sarcastically.

"I pardon you," said the fake Caliph's daughter to Siah. "You may come into the palace so that I can put my ring on your finger and make . . . the entire horizon . . . horizons . . . kneel before you." The lover moved to stand beside Siah and whispered: "Please go, I beg you." Siah went inside. He saw the manager, who was more upset than before. "Why are you doing this?" he asked.

"Don't worry," Siah went on calmly. "I plan to change the play. I want to show there's a trick involved. The Caliph's daughter has sent her maid on purpose to get rid of the lover. But this idiot doesn't understand. Do you suppose the crowd is foolish enough to believe she's the real Caliph's daughter?"

"It's dark," said the manager. "How will they ever know?"

"How could they not know?" replied Siah, and came out. As he stepped through the palace door and onto the stage, he saw Juji Khan's litter, which his ministers were carrying on their shoulders. They brought in the barrow and set it down on the floor in front of the cardboard palace door, then drew the curtain. But Juji Khan remained seated and refused to come out. He was supposed to appear in the second act, not here in the street and in front of the palace's side door.

The lover was going berserk. Siah took a look at the barrow with Juji Khan inside and then glanced at the lover. "Hey, you wretched lover," he said, "hide yourself until I find out who this is. It's obvious he's a stranger. He's lost his way. Should he see you here and inform the Caliph, you're finished. 'They'll fill your straw with skin,' too, as the sister said." The lover disappeared behind the stage curtain. Siah walked toward the litter. He stuck his head inside and said: "Why did you come now?"

"Your words incited me to come," said Juji Khan softly. "If I hadn't come now, then I would never be able to come."

"Then stand up and step out," said Siah. "If you don't do it now you never will." Siah took his hand and brought him out. He practically pulled him out. It didn't seem like he had any will of his own. Siah bowed and said, "Sir, who might you be, passing by the Caliph's palace?"

Juji Khan watched Siah silently. He said nothing.

"Sir, from your appearance it would seem that you don't speak our language. Or perhaps you can't speak at all."

Juji Khan said nothing.

"This handsome prince has come from China to ask for my hand," shouted the fake Caliph's daughter from the terrace. "He's the son of the exalted Chinese Empero . . . Emper . . ."

Siah didn't let her finish "Emperor." She wouldn't have been able to say it anyway. He said, "Hey, sister, you're imagining things. Where can you find a husband these days anyway?" Juji Khan laughed involuntarily. "Then you're not dumb?" asked Siah. "You're Chinese? No?"

Juji Khan nodded.

"Chin chun yung. Chian chung ching," said Siah aloud. This made Juji Khan laugh along with the audience. "Chian chang chung," Siah continued.

Juji Khan seemed to have forgotten where he was. Still laughing, he said, "You know how to talk nonsense very well."

"I'm not talking nonsense, brother. You know our language, too, then? I thought you were a stranger. Have you lost your way?"

Juji Khan opened his arms and stepped forward, and without being scared, said: "I am a stranger in love; which is the path?"

"Which path are you talking about?"

Juji Khan fell silent again. The fake Caliph's daughter called from the terrace; "Are you seeking the path to the palace of the Caliph of Baghdad? I am the Caliph's daughter's nurse. I will take you to the girl tonight for five dinars."

Siah appreciated the woman's timely cooperation and said: "Hail to you, nurse. You did well to fool the lover and get rid of him. Bravo. But don't you feel sorry for this young man? You are sending him to his death."

Juji Khan raised his arms again and stepped forward to say. "I am a passerby, I have no affair with the Caliph's daughter. I am a passenger who has been left behind by the convoy and has lost his way. I resemble a flower grown in the sand, thirsting for water. I had waited far too long, when suddenly a hand came forth, cut me from the sand, set me in a vase and watered me; only then was I able to bloom . . ."

Siah cut Juji Khan off and said. "Sir, you resemble the 'Shah Abdol Azim steam car.' You start late, but when you do start you never stop."

"Siah, the hand was yours. Your hand must be kissed." And he bent forward to kiss Siah's hand. Siah pulled himself back and asked: "Brother, when you were in the sand, did you perhaps get too much sun on your head?"

Juji Khan laughed and said: "It was dawn; the convoy chief gave the call: 'Rise, as it is late. Others have left and already reached their destinations. We have a long way ahead of us.' I heard the caravan's bell, but sleep would not allow me to open my eyes. Siah, you were the one who awakened me and succeeded to move me . . ."

"Dear sir, your brakes have failed again," said Siah. "You haven't said which path you're seeking."

"I seek the path to Kaaba. Won't you be my guide?"

"Sir, I don't know the path to Kaaba myself. I do know, though, that it's a long ways yet. This is only Baghdad, the first stop. Hey, brother, are you a Moslem too? What a mess!" Siah laughed and his laughter was lost in the crowd's.

Until then, Juji Khan's companions, who had brought him to the stage in the barrow, were standing cross-armed and silent. One of them, playing the role of the Chinese prince's advisor, stepped forward. He bowed to Juji Khan and said: "Sire, I urge you to consider remaining in Baghdad for a while and rest, and you could have an audience with the Caliph." He turned toward Siah and added: "And you, eunuch of the Caliph's court, may announce the time for the audience."

Siah placed his hands over his eyes and said; "Certainly."

"The purpose of this endless journey with all its suffering was indeed to meet with you, old man of wisdom," said Juji Khan. "I no longer have any business either in Baghdad or with its Caliph."

The nurse spoke up from the terrace: "Young man, at least make up your mind about the Caliph's daughter. She's a girl created for God's sight alone. She's a girl whose beauty surpasses the full moon's."

"Nurse, is this girl created only for lovemaking?" yelled Juji Khan angrily.

The nurse pointed to the palace, which was nonexistent, and said: "Well, the girl gets bored in this huge palace; what else can she do but make love? Young man, be a gentleman and ask for her hand."

"Is it by force?" screamed Juji Khan furiously. "Is the ruler's order 'Off with his head?' No, I must continue with my search for my intended goal this very night." And he walked toward the barrow. Before Siah could reach him, he was seated in the litter. Siah thrust his head inside again and said quietly: "You fool. There're two more acts to go. Where do you think you're going?"

"I'm going and I am ashamed of my hard-headedness," said Juji Khan aloud from inside the litter.

Siah lost hope in Juji Khan. He addressed the advisor and the other companions of the Chinese prince who were about to leave: "Don't you go too far from Baghdad. His majesty's audience is early tomorrow morning. Don't force me to have His Majesty the Caliph punish this young man in such a way that they will write it in story books." And astonished he looked in amazement at Juji Khan who had left the litter on his own. He came toward Siah and said; "Pardon me. Have pity on my youth."

"Did your engine stall?" asked Siah.

The first curtain fell after Siah's repeated signals. Somehow they continued through the other two acts. In the second act His Majesty the Caliph, with Siah and the Nurse's mediation, pardoned Juji Khan. Poor Juji Khan had to make love to the Caliph's daughter's other nurse during the entire fifteen minutes of the third act. It was Siah's idea to cover the nurse's face so that only her bright black eyes could be seen, and it worked. And justly Juji Khan bestowed upon her the title 'My veiled Idol.'

The show was over. The audience was gone. The actors were gone. Only Siah remained behind in the playhouse, washing off the black; Juji Khan waited for him on the bench. Laughing, he repeatedly told Siah, who was wiping his face "Thank you; thanks a lot." Siah hung his cape on the nail, and Juji Khan stood up. "Mohsen said you always get everyone going," he said, "but you can't believe it until you see it for yourself. Mohsen is a good friend. He can stay sick for a while, until I fully get going." Siah was silent and looked for his jacket. Juji Khan talked non-stop. "I only want to ask you whether you really know what you're doing? Do you say these things on purpose? You said a few heavy, dangerous words in there. You really handled the play with expertise. You're indeed the greatest actor I've ever seen." Siah put on his jacket. He looked in the mirror and said: "The black never washes off completely."

"Let's go," said Juji Khan. "You promised we'd eat dinner together tonight. My house is not too far. If you want, we could even take a taxi."

They set out. The lights in the theater had been turned off, and the street was deserted. They crossed to the sidewalk on the other side. A woman who wore a black veil and had carefully covered her face sat underneath a tree in the dark. When she saw them, she stood up and quietly said:

"Agha Mehdi."

They both turned, and Siah recognized her. She was the Caliph's daughter.

"Dear girl," said Siah, "why didn't you show up tonight? We had a hell of a time to pull the play off. Don't you realize we can't get by without you?"

The girl walked along with them, and Siah introduced the actors to each other.

"Had it not been for Agha Mehdi's expertise," said Juji Khan, "your not turning up would have shut down the theatre again, especially with my inexperience."

"I almost died this afternoon," said the girl, continuing to walk along beside them. "I have just come from the doctor's office—" Then she turned to Mehdi and went on,

"—Agha Mehdi, can I speak with you alone?" Juji Khan quickened his pace; Siah and the girl stopped.

"Dear Siah," said the girl, "God bless you, you must do me two favors. I have no one to turn to but you. First, you mustn't let me lose my job . . ."

"You can be sure of that," interrupted Siah.

"And the other is this," the girl continued. "You must gather at least two hundred *tomans* for me tonight, any way you can."

"Two hundred *tomans*? What do you want all that money for?"

"Siah dear, I have to go to the doctor tomorrow to get rid of the child. I have taken the shot tonight; if I don't go tomorrow, my life will be in danger."

"Look girl, you know better," Siah said helplessly. "Even if I did my very best, I could perhaps come up with thirty or forty *tomans* maximum."

"How about this friend of yours? Can't you borrow it from him? He looks well off."

"Don't even think about it," croaked Siah. "If I borrow from him, he'll think . . ."

"In this indecent world, only you want to remain decent?" said the girl irritably. "I have nothing to say to you anymore. Call your friend." And then she started to walk quickly. The three came together and passed through the deserted streets. The girl had no intention of saying goodbye. She talked intimately with Juji Khan, laughed, and once even took his hand. But she distanced herself from Siah. She pretended to be offended. They reached the house. Juji Khan thrust his hand in his pocket and found his keys. He opened the door and said:

"Please come in." Then he looked at the girl, who had just stood there. "You can come in too if you would like."

"Agha Mehdi never goes anywhere," said the girl coquettishly. "He must really be fond of you to have come tonight," and as they went in the house, she said, "I'm glad to get to know my future fellow player."

They entered the room which seemed strange to Siah. There was a large desk in the middle of the room and two full bookcases on each side of the desk. There was a sculpture on the table. Juji Khan turned on the table lamp, and it lit up the face of the sculpture. The sculpture seemed to be both laughing and crying. It was both a man and a woman. It was nude and sat comfortably cross-legged. A black cat with blue eyes walked into the room. It went directly to Juji Khan, rubbed itself against his leg and meowed. The girl bent down, picked up the cat and kissed it. "Sweet kitty, you're hungry?" she said. "Or are you in love, too? Perhaps you fancy your master?" Siah saw that the cat scratched the girl's hand, but she pretended nothing had happened. She continued to hold the cat in her arms. She petted its head, ears, and neck.

"Please sit down," said Juji Khan. "I'll go and bring something to eat."

As he was leaving the room, he called out; "Ahmad," and a voice replied from somewhere; "Yes, sir."

Siah and the girl sat on two couches which were next to each other in the corner of the room. There was a table in front of them. The girl let go of the cat and swore:

"The damned thing bloodied my hand."

A thick book was stuck to the wall opposite them with a large nail. A photograph of the sole of a foot was pinned to the same wall next to the book. For a second, Siah was about to get up and see what book it was, but he didn't feel like it. He was too downhearted.

"The only person in front of whom I feel ashamed is you," said the girl.

"Why do you want to abort the child anyway?" asked Mehdi kindly. "Have mercy."

"Dear Siah, it's as if you don't live in this world. How can I work with a child? How can I earn a living?"

"The person who planted the child in you should pay the price."

The girl sneered and said, "He's got a wife and kids. He left me as soon as he found out I was pregnant."

"That simple? Wasn't he going to marry you?" asked Siah.

"No, he never said he'd marry me. Siah dear, you're very naive and decent. You think everybody's like yourself."

Siah thought for a while and said: "Dear girl, can't you find a decent man and marry him? Settle down? Isn't it a pity to get yourself constantly into trouble like this? You're cutting off your own roots."

"Which decent man will marry me?" the girl replied. "Supposing he did anyway; the first thing he'd say is, 'I don't want you to step outside the house. I don't like you to act in the theater.' "

"It's not important, dear girl; acting on the stage isn't all that important. The main thing is to pull off one's life correctly."

The girl seemed irritated and tired of this conversation. "Siah dear, my situation is past this kind of talk," she said.

"No matter how, I must find two hundred *tomans* from somewhere tonight. I know how myself. But it's only that I'm ashamed in front of you. Will you permit me? Will you permit me . . . your friend?"

Siah stood up; he couldn't cry there. He wished to go home and cry his heart out. Even if he cried as much as all the rain in the world, it would still not be enough. When one is struck so deep to have to go so low, how it must break one's heart. It's just like spitting in one's own face. The poor girl. Siah had always seen her from afar, with her oak-colored hair covering her shoulders, those huge black eyes which broke one's heart to look at; with those lips and mouth which opened like a blossom and from which the stars poured out onto one's lap; those eyebrows which always seemed to beckon to share a secret which one didn't understand. And such a girl has had pity on no part of herself. He wished he could go and see nothing, hear nothing, want nothing.

The girl begged: "Siah dear, don't walk around the room so much. Come and sit down. I'm getting nauseous." Siah sat down, and the girl started over again: "Give me permission, my dear Siah. I have no other choice. My life is at stake. If you can get it, I'll be more than willing to leave right now and not feel so ashamed in front of you. I have an appointment tomorrow morning. The shot he's given me rips the child into pieces; tomorrow I have to go so that he can pull it out. You have no idea how painful it is. I have already done it four times. The way he scratches the inside with his pincers darkens the world before my eyes. I pray to die tomorrow during the operation, so that you won't have to look at me this way. Are you satisfied now?"

Siah wished he had the money. He wished he could find the two hundred *tomans* that very same night. He wished, as the girl had said, he was not a decent man in this indecent world and could ask Juji Khan for the money.

He saw the girl take off her veil, bundle it up, and throw it in the corner. She opened her purse, took out a comb and lipstick. She put them on the arm of the couch. She took out a mirror and quickly put on the lipstick and pressed her lips together. She combed her hair, opened the buttons of her blouse and adjusted her bra, but did not close all the buttons. She had changed. But her face was empty. Siah asked:

"You've put your make-up on?"

Juji Khan came in with a tray on which there was a bottle, a few cups, and a dish of salad. He placed the tray on the desk. Behind him a man walked in wearing pajama bottoms, a woolen shirt, and a knit cap. He said hello and placed a dish with two broiled chickens on the table. The man left and came back with more things, setting them down neatly.

Juji Khan sat behind the desk.

It's going to start now, Siah thought to himself. They're standing before each other like two drunken cats.

The girl stood up. She moved her hips and waist as if she was on stage. She said:

"Allow me to become the cupbearer."

She picked up the bottle and looked at it. She asked: "Is it whiskey?" and she laughed. She filled a cup and put it in front of Juji Khan. Then she poured some for Siah. She didn't look at him as she placed the cup on the arm of the couch. She poured herself less than the others. Her eyes were gleaming, but not like when she made love on stage.

She hit her cup against Juji Khan's and said:

"To your health."

She took a leaf of lettuce from the salad dish and put it in her mouth. She laughed again, but falsely. Even her nurses on the stage laughed more easily than she did. She attacked the chicken, placing each person's share on the plates and setting the plate before each one. She sat on the corner of the desk. The light on the desk lit only her arm and her skirt, not her exposed breasts. Sitting on the desk, she moved her legs about and laughed. She began to sing. Her voice was hoarse and uninspired. She sang the same song Siah expected her to sing: "Had there been only one pain, there'd be no problem." This was the same girl who used to sing before the play started, and Siah would accompany her with a tambourine. Oh, how the two of them aroused the audience and how, when the song had ended and they had left the stage, the crowd clapped for them to return. The girl asked Juji Khan:

"Is there a tambourine or something else to be found in this house?"

"I don't know how to play," said Juji Khan.

"Agha Mehdi does," she said. "He can even play the violin."

"No, I don't have a tambourine," said Juji Khan.

The girl continued her song, and Siah felt she was forcing herself to sing. Perhaps she was ill again. Siah started to eat. The girl left her song unfinished. Like a person who has just awakened, she asked Juji Khan:

"Am I going to wake your parents?"

"No, they sleep upstairs. Even if they do wake up, they'll think I'm listening to the radio."

The girl laughed again. She narrowed her eyes and fixed them on Juji Khan. She cut a leg of the chicken with a fork and bent toward Juji Khan. Juji Khan didn't open his mouth. He took the fork and said:

"Thank you."

The girl searched in her plate and found a wish bone. She held it before Juji Khan and said:

"Should we make a bet?"

"For what?"

"For a kiss."

Juji Khan bit his lips and lowered his head. The girl said:

"What a bashful little boy."

Siah stood up. He got up so abruptly that the cup on the arm of the couch fell on the carpet. It didn't break, just emptied its contents. He said:

"Why don't you two bet for money? For two hundred *tomans*, cash?"

Bronze female figurine with Ibex
Iran, Luristan; 8th century B.C.

Traitor's Intrigue

Until yesterday, it had been sunny and warm, but this morning the sky was suddenly cast in bronze; the cold weather and metallic sky weighed heavily on the heart. Every year, no matter which orderly they had, by now he would have installed stoves in the rooms, moved the flower pots to the greenhouse, set wooden boards over the blue mosaic pool, heaped the fallen leaves on the boards, and washed the yard clean. This year however, the colonel's retirement had disrupted everything.

Holding a pigeon in his arms, Keyvan came onto the porch. "You missed school again, child," the colonel said.

"Grandpa, my pigeon isn't feeling well," Keyvan replied. "Besides, the school bus didn't honk more than once."

The Colonel took the pigeon from Keyvan. Its body was warm, but the eyes were shut, and the head was drooping

over its chest. "Grandpa, let's take it to the doctor," Keyvan
said. "Otherwise, I'll start to cry again." Then he went on.
"I'll wake up in the middle of the night, put on my
clothes, take my piggy bank, go out the front gate, and
walk, all by myself, to my mother. Then I'll get lost and
you'll be sorry, and no matter how much you search you
won't find me."

The colonel's life was bound to this small child. He had
told his daughter, now that she was divorced, to stay at her
father's house and raise her child. Instead, the girl had
cashed in her trousseau and with her dowry and her
thirty-seven gold coins had left for Germany. She had
declared, "I shall study hairdressing and trap myself a
German husband too. Just watch!" Well, Mansoureh
Khanoum adored Keyvan too. And they had an orderly as
well. Every two years the colonel rummaged through the
conscripts' files and picked out the best ones. He would
then send them straight to the medical center. He believed
the Yazdis[9] would become the most hardworking; the
Shirazis[10] the most witty and eloquent, and the Turks the
most dutiful orderlies. Crazy Fatemeh too, would always
appear when you needed her, asking, "What can I do?"
The kids in the street had nicknamed her, when she was
still young, "Brigitte Bardot." Mansoureh Khanoum used
to say, "She bleaches her hair with hydrogen peroxide,
that's why it's become frizzy."

Fatemeh washed clothes well and ironed even better.
And now, on the first day of winter, Fatemeh was probably

---

[9]Yazdis: people from Yazd, a central province of Iran.

[10]Shirazis: people from Shiraz, a southern city of Iran.

sitting under her warm *korsy*,[11] knitting washcloths to sell for a living. No more the days of orderlies or of being called "Colonel, Sir." Even Mansoureh Khanoum had now gone on strike and had not gotten out of bed. She had declared, "I shall not leave the bed until the stoves are installed and the house is warm." Even young, she wasn't much. She would either pray and fast or read useless books and deny the colonel his sleep. She woke him up every time she turned the pages. And the lamp on her night table was always lit. The colonel woke up at six every morning. He exercised first, ran around the yard three times, had breakfast, and then left, not returning until evening. The first person who realized that the colonel had actually retired was Mansoureh Khanoum—and how! She began to complain about his being constantly in the way, always at home, roaming from one room to another like a wandering ghost, either playing solitaire or puffing away on cigarettes. She insisted that the colonel find another job and quit smoking. She would tell him, "Let's go travel in our final days. Let's go to magnificent Mecca, to the high thresholds."

The colonel took Keyvan's hand. It was freezing. They left the house with the pigeon under Keyvan's arm. He thought to himself, "I'll go to Haji[12] Ali, the stove-maker, on the corner of Asadi Avenue. The pigeon will surely be dead by the time we get there. We'll throw it on the garbage pile beside the street. Hopefully, with Haji Ali's help, we'll

---

[11]*Korsy*: a low, square table with a thick cloth overhanging on all sides. A brazier with hot coals is placed under the table.

[12]Haji: title given to a man who has made the pilgrimage to Mecca.

distract the child." Haji Ali had two wives and a squadron of children. He knew how to sweet talk his wives and children. "But for me, a retired colonel, no one gives a hoot any more, neither my wife, nor my grandson, and not even Crazy Fatemeh." They hadn't reached Haji Ali's shop when he saw the *Sagha-khaneh*[13] drinking fountain across from the mosque. On top of the fountain there was a platform across which was a vault-like structure. Portraits of holy men were set up here and there on the vault, and a green ribbon was twisted all around them. Half-burnt candles were scattered over the platform. Right across the mosque sat a man with a brown cloak and *shab-kolah*.[14] A brazier of burning coal was in front of him and he was reciting the Koran. The colonel told Keyvan, "Go and place your pigeon on the fountain platform. God will cure it."

He couldn't have had a better idea. The child set out running. The colonel followed stiffly. Keyvan stood on his toes and placed his pigeon on the platform. He said, "But Grandpa, we don't have candles."

The man reciting the Koran raised his head and said, "If it is a corpse, it is impure, take it away."

The colonel glanced at the man. He had a pale face with almost colorless eyes; his lips had even less color. His cloak and tunic were old, but clean. The colonel deepened his

---

[13]*Sagha-khaneh*: a small public watering place where passersby may help themselves to a cool drink. It is to be found in the older sections of every town and village in Iran. It is set up usually in a recessed niche—with its cistern and brass bowl—as a good religious deed in memory of Imam Hosayn, the third Shi'ite imam who was martyred with his followers at Karbala (in present-day Iraq) in a battle with the forces of Yazid, the Omayyad ruler in 61/680 in the course of two hot waterless days. (Encyclopaedia Iranica)

[14]*Shab-kolah*: a cap usually worn under a turban.

voice, forgetting he was in civilian clothes, and retorted, "It's none of your business, worthless scum." Then he took a two-rial coin from his pocket, gave it to Keyvan and said, "Here, my son. Give it to the nosy beggar for the love of God."

Keyvan offered the coin in his small palm. The man didn't take it. The colonel said furiously, "Keyvan, throw it in front of him."

Haji Ali stepped out of his shop. The merchant and his apprentice, from the fruit stand next to the water fountain, also came out and gathered around them. Two pedestrians stopped as well. Haji Ali, his face black from smoke, rubbed his sooty hands on his trousers, buttoned his jacket over his large belly and said, "Colonel, sir, it's not like you. I heard you call the Agha[15] a beggar. In the entire Tajrish area, we have only the Agha to be grateful for."

The cloaked man raised his head from the Koran and said, 'I *am* a beggar. A beggar at the door of Imam Ali and all the innocent ones."

The colonel laughed. He was about to say "Stop babbling!" But he realized that they were six and he was alone. He could never take them on, even though he knew Haji Ali well. Every time Mansoureh Khanoum cooked *ashe-e reshteh* soup or *halva*[16] they sent him a bowl or a plate of it. Of course, that was until last year, when they still had an orderly. Haji Ali took the pigeon from the water

---

[15] Agha: literally means "sir"; also used to address respected clergymen.

[16] *Ash-e reshteh*: a thick noodle and bean soup; *halva* is a sweet dish, commonly prepared on religious occasions.

fountain platform. The pigeon's head was hanging. He said, "Young man, you've clipped the pigeon's wings. It hasn't been able to fly and has died of cold."

"I didn't clip them. Grandpa did." said Keyvan.

"Pigeons fly but always return to their coops," said Haji Ali. He took Keyvan's hand and continued "Young man, let's go to the municipal garden and bury it next to the seedlings. Mr. Avakh, the gardener, is my friend."

Keyvan's tears covered his face. The colonel was tempted to pull off the man's cloak from his shoulders and his *shab-kolah* from his head and trample on them. Too bad he didn't have his boots on.

In the afternoon, Haji Ali came to the house, and the colonel was compelled to lend him a hand. Installing five stoves is no joke and the rooms were freezing cold, too. As evening approached, the work was finished and Haji Ali fired up all the stoves. They roared. Keyvan had been getting along with Haji Ali, following him from room to room, handing him the rag and the enamel bowl, and rushing to the kitchen to fetch him matches.

Mansoureh Khanoum brought Haji Ali some tea. He complained, "I missed my noon and evening prayers."

"You should've said your prayers before you started to work," said Mansoureh Khanoum. "You were sure to find both a prayer cloth and the *Qiblah*[17] in this house."

When Mansoureh Khanoum left, the colonel asked Haji Ali, "Who was that good-for-nothing bum who upset us first thing this morning? If I'd had my car, I would have run him over."

---

[17]*Qiblah*: the direction toward which Moslems turn to pray.

"Colonel, sir, don't talk like that," said Haji Ali. "The Agha has hundreds of devoted followers, some like yourself and many even more important than you."

"This contemptible mullah?" asked the Colonel.

"Sir, I have eaten your bread and salt many times. Otherwise, in the name of Morteza Ali,[18] I would never have stepped into this house."

He didn't touch his tea and continued, "The Agha is the prayer leader at the Asadi Mosque. He also goes behind the pulpit and preaches. They have banned him from both."

"Who has banned him?"

"You know better!"

"What has he done?"

"I was there the day they arrested him. He was preaching from the pulpit, 'People of Islam, all this blood shed in the cause of truth has not been wasted. It is boiling in the hearts of you and me.' Of course, I can't remember the exact words, but he was saying, 'Don't ask me why I say, long live . . . or death to . . . The noble Koran has been my mentor. So I announce: Hail to Abraham, whose purpose was to build, and may the two hands of Abi Lahab[19] be cut off, as he was a hypocrite and a coward.' Of course, he was there reciting verses in Arabic and interpreting them, and how the crowd was moved! He cursed Abi Lahab and all the likes of him in the world. He was saying outright, 'Death to . . .' Well, obviously

---

[18]Morteza: "approved"; "Morteza Ali" is the manner in which reference is made to the Imam Ali.

[19]Abi Lahab: an adversary of the Prophet Mohammad.

they hung his turban around his neck and . . ."

The colonel interrupted Haji Ali and asked, "How does he make a living now?"

"People haven't forsaken him."

"Well, from what I gather, he is sitting across from the mosque, begging."

"No, dear sir. His home is the source of hope for the people. They go to his door. He is sitting across from the mosque just to spite *them*. He says, 'Here is my fort.' "

"Does he have a family?"

"A wife and three children."

"Why should a person with a family create so much trouble for himself?"

"People take care of his family, too."

"But why should he force his own family to beg?"

"His wife is a lioness. After Agha got into trouble, I went to their house. I saw a pile of dirty clothes in front of her. It was the neighbors'. I rushed back home and sent both my wives to help her."

"Are your wives united? I have only one and can't even handle her!"

"Your wife, sir, is a gem," said Haji Ali. "Of course, I mean this in a brotherly way. She really cares for people, especially for the families of prisoners."

The colonel stroked his moustache and said, "Yes, you were saying . . ."

"Anyhow, by evening the women had washed all the clothes, cleaned the rooms, and wiped the windows. Later they described how in the afternoon a crowd had descended upon the house. One person had brought rice, others cooking oil, squash, sugar, tea, cereal, even bread and meat *choub-khat*.[20] They said one of the devotees had brought a sack full of eggplant and a woman office employee had brought a bottle of tranquilizers."

"What did she do with all that eggplant?"

"The Agha's wife is fair. She took just enough for their own use and divided the rest among the poor families."

Keyvan hadn't uttered a word until then. His teacher had instructed him to write out three pages of the phrase "man is human." He hadn't done his homework the night before last. He sat next to the stove writing, then he busied himself, cleaning his gun. The colonel had taken him to Tajrish Bridge around noon to amuse him and make him forget his pigeon. He had bought him a pair of woolen gloves and an umbrella. Later, he had taken him to the toy store and, on Keyvan's insistence, had bought him a toy air gun, on condition that he didn't aim at his cat. He had taught him how to polish the gun, where to place the pellet, and how to aim. Keyvan's cat was now sleeping next to the stove, and its eyes were closed. Keyvan set the gun aside and asked, "Haji Ali, does this man have any children my age?"

"His eldest son is your age, young man," replied Haji Ali.

"Is he in the first grade? Which school does he go to?"

"An Islamic school, young man. All our children go to Islamic schools."

"My name is Keyvan," he said. "You keep calling me 'young man.' "

Mansoureh Khanoum came into the sitting room and exclaimed, "Eh, Haji Ali, your tea is cold!"

---

[20]*Choub-khat*: a piece of wood serving the same purpose as a credit account.

Haji Ali said, "Madame, in the name of the *Kaaba*'s black holy stone, which I've kissed, and with neighbor's rights, I will not touch another morsel of your bread and salt unless the colonel apologizes to the Agha."

Mansoureh Khanoum picked up the cat from beside the stove, sat in its place, and said, "First of all, tea doesn't have salt."

She contemplated for a second, then asked, "What has he done this time? Since he's retired, he picks on everyone like a fighting cock."

"You go and do your crossword puzzle, fry your eggplants, and leave the thinking to men," said the colonel.

"He hasn't delivered the papers yet," said Mansoureh. "This delivery business is going to drive us mad. One day he delivers, the next he doesn't."

Haji Ali rose, put on his jacket and buttoned it up. The colonel got up too, reached into his pocket and brought out a bundle of notes. Haji Ali asked, "Colonel, sir, when are you going to come, so we can go together?"

"Do you want them to cut off my pittance of a pension?" asked the colonel.

It took the colonel three days to finally get hold of Mr. Avakh, the municipal gardener. It was eleven o'clock in the morning in the Soleimani dairy shop. The colonel, putting on his usual air, instructed. "For the time being you can choose the site for the plants; start work tomorrow at six in the morning." Passing through Asadi Avenue, they reached the mosque. The holy man was still sitting in the same spot. Greeting him, Mr. Avakh bent forward and kissed his hand. The colonel involuntarily said hello. The man didn't reply; he looked up and said something in

Arabic, of which the colonel understood only the word "traitors." Haji Ali rushed out of his shop. He said excitedly, "Agha, the colonel has come to apologize. Didn't you say from the pulpit that there is repentance in religion?"

The colonel was fuming with rage. He wished he could beat up the three of them. But the strength of youth was no longer there. He shouted out at Haji Ali, "Be sensible man. When did I ever say I'd come to apologize?"

As if mocking a child, Haji Ali said, "Kiss Agha's hand, sir."

"I refuse to even kiss my ancestor's hand, let alone this lousy mullah's," said the colonel.

He stopped himself from saying anything else, especially since they were three and he was alone. What if they jumped on him? The cloaked man was spindly, but Haji Ali and Mr. Avakh were tough and stocky. When forces are not equal, one either retreats or uses war tactics. Fortunately, Haji Ali turned and went back to his shop. Mr. Avkah, too, returned the same way he had come. The cloaked man threw out a verse in Arabic.

The colonel went home and sat in the sitting room in a filthy mood. Well done, thanks a lot. A measly mullah doesn't respond to one's salutation, curses in Arabic which one can't even understand.

If only he weren't retired he'd know what to do with the mullah. "Traitors? Me, a traitor? I, who have served the government for thirty years? Of course, I didn't fly once, even though I was an air force officer. But is office work not work? From dawn to dusk, one has to put up with all sorts of good and bad, and then stagnate for fifteen years as a colonel, waiting from one year to the next, hoping to be promoted to the rank of general. To keep studying every year, military tactics, topography, world strategy—even learn English, at this age, and still not get a promotion, but retirement instead. All the while one's previous subordinates become commanders and generals, and you have to lift your hand to salute them. With all these sorrows and then to be called a 'traitor'! I'll teach him. How about sending a few soldiers with clubs, in civilian clothes, to beat him good and proper? But I'm retired. Still, I can phone Sergeant Ayvaz-zadeh and tell him to arrange the job. As a matter of fact, why the hell is this man sitting there, obstructing the way? 'I shall not forsake my fort!' he says. What fort? Fortification is for war time, and only soldiers fortify to take cover."

He took off his shoes, threw them at the doorway, and yelled, "Ay, bring my slippers!" He picked up the playing cards which were on top of the radio and played various solitaire games, but couldn't calm down. He busied himself with his prayer beads. That didn't help either. It had been three months since he'd quit smoking. That was no easy task. In the meantime, he'd consumed a lot of roasted almonds, candy, and chewing gum. He went to the cabinet and took out a pack of Winston's. His hands were shaking as he opened it. He had no matches. He yelled out, "Are there no matches to be found in this house?"

Mansoureh Khanoum did not reply. She was probably saying her noontime prayers and would then read the Book of Fourth Imam, and by then it was time for her evening prayers. He went into the kitchen barefoot, found the matches and came back. He wasted three matches before finally lighting his cigarette.

Mansoureh Khanoum came in. She asked, "What is it with you?"

She saw the smoke rings and exclaimed, "Eh! You are smoking again! Wasn't it you who promised you'd never touch another cigarette?"

"Leave me in peace, woman," the colonel retorted. "I said hello to a mullah across from the Asadi Mosque and he totally ignored me. The day Keyvan's pigeon died, he insulted me and the boy in front of everyone. Today he cursed me in Arabic. Why the hell should he be allowed to curse in a language I don't understand?" And he yelled out, "The measly, lousy good-for-nothing!"

Mansoureh Khanoum asked, "I hope it wasn't Agha Sheik Abdullah, the prayer leader of the mosque? He was in prison for a while. He is now banned from the mosque and the pulpit."

"That's him. Do you know him? I'll teach him what an Agha is."

Mansoureh Khanoum sat next to the colonel, rested her hands on her knees and said, "Enough—don't pretend to be so aloof, asking me whether I know him. I used to pray behind him. When he served time in prison, I visited his wife and children."

"I see, I see, you too, old woman . . ."

"I told you that I help the families of prisoners . . ."

"Yes, you told me, but not that you helped these useless types."

"*You* are the useless one. Let me tell you I haven't given away any of your money. Most of it comes from despotism, dear."

"Now that I'm retired even you have learned to answer

back? Watch it, or I'll break your bones."

"You are taking out your frustrations on me," answered
Mansoureh Khanoum quietly, "but I'm not going to argue
with you now. Remember, I'm not your foe. We have put
up with each other for thirty years. Don't worry if the
Agha hasn't responded to your greeting. Say hello a second,
a third, even a tenth time. It's the likes of you that have
caused him all this misfortune."

"Woman, this man is opposing the government," said the
colonel. "I, on the other hand, earn my living from the
government. You expect me to go and kiss his hand? Say
hello to him again? Not in a hundred years. Let him
dream on."

"You will because you're not an evil man at heart," said
Mansoureh Khanoum. "Be assured the Agha divides all the
Islamic taxes between the families of the poor. His own
family lives modestly on a *ziloo*."[21]

"Why is he demeaning himself? Why? Why is he sitting
across from the mosque in this bitter cold weather? Is there
nowhere else to go? Why doesn't he just sit in his own
home?"

"He's probably got the endurance," said Mansoureh
Khanoum. "In his heart he knows he's right. He has faith."

The colonel became quiet all of a sudden. He looked at
his wife and felt sorry for her. Her hair had grown white.
It was impossible to count the lines around her eyes and
lips. Even her cheeks were covered with wrinkles. The
dimple on her left cheek, which had appeared every time
she smiled when she was young, was now a deep line. She

---

[21]*Ziloo*: pileless carpet.

had gained weight. Her knees were swollen. Her fingers were puffy. This woman had lived with him for thirty years. She had borne him three sons and a daughter, all of whom were now scattered in different towns or countries. They wrote letters to their mother, who would put on her glasses and sit down to read them several times. They sent their regards to their father. This woman had shared the same pillow with him for thirty years, had caressed him with love, compassion and sympathy. She had cared for him in sickness; prepared his meals. Yes, she had told him that she took care of the families of the prisoners, but she hadn't told him which prisoners. It was the colonel's own fault. He was always so tired after work. And in the morning, he was up at six. For what? For whom? So that the likes of that mullah could ignore him and for his wife to tell him it was the likes of him who brought the Agha misfortune? Well I'll be damned. He was accustomed to the bitter tongue of his wife, but still . . .

The colonel would have his dinner, then sit in front of the television and fall asleep right there. His wife would gently touch him on the shoulder and say "Wake up, dear. Go to bed and sleep. You'll catch cold here."

She would take his arm and, after he was in bed, cover him with the quilt and ask, "Would you like me to rub your feet?"

His wife was always awake before him. She said her prayers and made sure the colonel didn't leave the house before having breakfast. She'd squeeze fresh fruit juice for him. Her eyes smiled as she looked at him. No question, from time to time they quarreled and his wife used bitter words. It was always she though, who came forward first to make up, always saying, "How much longer do you think we'll live?"

The colonel wasn't a bad husband either. Was it not his wife who had said earlier "You are not an evil man at heart?" He would not allow anything to trouble his family. Every year they vacationed by the sea. On the first of the month, he would take his wife to the military supermarket where, using his grocery booklet, he would do the shopping for the month. And he would carry all the bags to the car himself.

When he was young, friends nicknamed him "Lady-killer." Looking at himself in the mirror, he would curl his moustache. The air force uniform was very becoming, and his wife constantly burned wild rue to cast away the evil eye. Rolling his eyes, he would stare at his wife who would call him "Big Nose!" Yes, his nose was a bit too long, but he had a rather angular face, large black eyes, a thin moustache, and he was brisk and swift.

As he climbed into his jeep, Sudabeh Khanoum, the neighbor's wife, would rush out of her house and coquettishly ask for a ride to the bank or to the workers' clinic. She would purse her lips, brush the hair off her forehead and say, "Right here!" And then there was Fatemeh. Wherever the colonel was, she would suddenly appear in front of him. She would greet him, photographing him from head to toe with her eyes. In the blink of an eye all three of them had grown old—Fatemeh, his wife, and himself.

Beside Sudabeh Khanoum and Fatemeh, even Parvaneh, the young and lovely daughter of Mr. Mansouri, had told Mansoureh Khanoum outright that "I want a husband just like the colonel." But then he had remained a colonel for fifteen years. His own wife, Mansoureh Khanoum, however, wore the chador[22] and refused to wear make-up. Lately, she had even stopped plucking her eyebrows. She washed her face clean. That's all. And naturally, she considered nail polish religiously prohibited. She never accompanied the colonel to receptions. In the beginning of their marriage, she had attended one or two gatherings with him. But as soon as the playing cards were produced, she opened a book on the history of Sufism in Islam by Dr. Ghassem Ghani and began to read. Meanwhile, the guests cracked roasted seeds, smoked cigarettes, and mocked her. Alcohol, too, was more than abundant. One evening, Mansoureh Khanoum had brought her knitting. When the guests started to tease her, she became upset, got up and said aloud, "I should be the one making fun of you. But I will not because your sins shall be yours alone. Thank God we won't be buried in the same grave. My duty is to let it be known, and I have."

She left. The colonel caught up with her halfway home, but not a word was spoken.

The colonel had originally intended to smoke at least three or four cigarettes, one after the other. He suddenly decided against it and put out the half-burnt cigarette he was holding.

"Now, that's a good man," said Mansoureh Khanoum. "You've noticed how much better you've felt since you stopped smoking? Even at your age, if you repent and don't smoke and neither drink alcohol nor gamble, you will live

---

[22]Chador: a long veil used to cover the head and worn by woman over their clothes.

for a hundred years."

"You call this life?" said the colonel.

He took his wife's hand. The veins were swollen; the back of her hand was covered with black and brown spots. These hands, at one time, had been as white as flower petals.

"Say your prayers and read the Koran," said Mansoureh Khanoum. "You cannot imagine what a world it is. Your soul will be refreshed."

The colonel said nothing. Mansoureh Khanoum continued "My *marja-e taqlid*,[23] the religious leader I follow . . ."

The colonel laughed, remembering the night of their wedding. Mansoureh Khanoum's father had joined their hands, read a whole bunch of prayers and verses from the Koran, given them advice and then again prayed for them and had finally placed a large envelope on their pillows. It was the title deed for a house in the Ab Sardar area; he had made a wedding gift of it to his daughter. For years they had lived in that house, it had brought them luck. Later, the colonel was able to buy their current house on Parvin Street, one of the side streets off Asadi Avenue. They had rented Mansoureh Khanoum's house to a Haji from the Bazaar. The colonel owed their new house to his wife's prudent economizing, as it is widely known, a gambler's pockets are eternally empty.

When everyone had left the bridal chamber, the "Ladykiller" lieutenant took his bride's hand and kissed it. Her hand was as soft and delicate as a flower. He had

---

[23]*Marja-e taqlid*: the source of imitation, one "whose words and deeds serve as a guide for those unable to exert 'independent judgment' "; Hamid Enayat, *Modern Islamic Political Thought* (London: Macmillan, 1982).

said, "Well, tell me . . ."

Mansoureh Khanoum had lowered her head and asked, "Who is your *marja-e taqlid*? Who do you follow?"

Her voice was soft, but shaky. The lieutenant had laughed and said, "Come now. Let's have a kiss for the time being. Come on and give me a kiss."

Mansoureh Khanoum had been hurt. She had fixed her offended look upon him, her eyes feverish.

The colonel returned from his daydreams. He took the pack of cigarettes, put it in the cabinet, and turned the lock.

Mansoureh Khanoum asked, "Do you want to read a pamphlet? I have most of Dr. Shariati's books. I have hand copied some myself. Ayatollah Taleqani . . ."

"Why?"

"Why what?"

"Why have you copied them?"

"Because his books are banned. There is a six-month prison sentence for anyone caught with even a single copy."

Mansoureh Khanoum sighed and continued, "He is in prison himself. So is Taleqani. I truly wish I had permission to go and visit them."

"Why would you want to go prison to visit them?"

"I wish to go and tell them, 'Greetings, gentlemen.' "

The colonel thought and said, "You know very well I can't stand these religious pures and impures, permitted and prohibited, do's and don't's and things like that."

"These are trifles; the principle is justice."

"All right," said the colonel. "I shall say my prayer from now on, only if you allow me to take four permanent wives and ninety-nine temporary ones."

"I told you, the principle is justice; as soon as you take

another wife, you shall break my heart and do me injustice."

In the morning the clouds were gone and a pale sun was able to shine through. A few migrating birds, left behind from their flock, flew by. "We're not so old yet that we cannot work," said Mansoureh Khanoum. "We can move the flower pots to the greenhouse ourselves."

They had no other choice. Mr. Avakh had put on airs and told Fatemeh, "I refuse to go; I have no obligation."

Even Fatemeh had said "My shoulder aches, but I'll come just to show that I am not ungrateful."

Fatemeh's eyelids were puffed up and her right eye twitched constantly. There remained no sign of her photographing with her eyes, nor of the smile which needed no lips. Fatemeh's look seemed to say "Everything is finished, gone."

Half of her hair had grown white; the other half was a dull yellow. All of it was frizzed up. Her head seemed too large, as if inflated.

First, the colonel had pulled out the dahlias and the gladioli from the flower bed. He buried them under the sand, in the corner of the greenhouse, so that he could replant them at the end of winter if they remained alive. They picked up the geranium pots from the edge of the flower bed and set them in rows in the middle of the yard. Keyvan handed Mansoureh Khanoum the smaller pots, and she cut off the yellow and frozen leaves and filled the pot with fresh soil. Fatemeh then handed them to the colonel so that he could place them on the stairs of the greenhouse.

Moving the verbena and jasmine troughs required the strength of youth, which they all lacked. So, they dragged the pots to the doorstep of the greenhouse. The colonel would gasp, "In the name of Ali," and pick them up with a jerk, one by one, and set them in a row on the greenhouse floor. There were a few irises which they placed in the guest room, the sitting room, and in the hallway. Fatemeh dipped a piece of cotton in olive oil and rubbed their wide leaves until they shone. There was no more room in the greenhouse for the ferns and the cacti. They placed them in decorative pots here and there in a room next to the guest room, which now looked more like a greenhouse. By now, there was a plant or flower pot in every available spot. They were so properly set according to height that one could hold a military review of them.

That night, neither of them could sleep. Mansoureh Khanoum's hand and the colonel's back were in pain. Around midnight, Mansoureh Khanoum left her bed and brought the colonel an aspirin, one of those which their daughter had sent from Germany. She took one, too. Later she heated an oilcloth and applied it to the colonel's back. Moaning, the colonel said, "I wish the girl was here in person, instead of her picture on the oilcloth." In the morning, Fatemeh came. Her neck was stiff and would absolutely not move, neither left nor right. Mansoureh Khanoum had tied an elastic wrist band around her own hand. She applied some cream to Fatemeh's neck, rubbed it in and said, "Now try to move your head."

"It doesn't move, Madame," complained Fatemeh.

"This neck is no good anymore," said the colonel mockingly. "You should sell it to the street peddler!"

And now, it was time someone dared undertake the task of watering the plants in the main greenhouse and the room next to the guest room. The colonel declared that he would take care of it himself. He did, and nothing drastic happened. Later, Mansoureh Khanoum said, with admiration, "Thank God the four pillars of your body are still healthy. God forbid the evil eye from being cast on you. Only your nose is too big. It almost reaches your chin now; it looks like a parrot's beak."

Thursday night, Mansoureh Khanoum had begun cooking the cereals for *ash-e reshteh*. The soup was ready by eleven o'clock Friday morning, and what a soup it was! She filled a bowl and decorated the top with fried mint, onions, garlic, minced meat, and saffron. "Drive us to the Agha's house," she told the colonel.

Keyvan climbed in too. The car was large, and the back alleys were narrow and covered with mud. At one point, the car's fender hit a lamppost by the wall, but the colonel didn't complain. Mansoureh Khanoum and Keyvan entered the house, carrying the bowl of *ash-e reshteh*. The colonel waited in the car. The alley was like a piece of fertile land of dirt and mud rolling in front of him. A group of kids, large and small, had set up a torn volleyball net and were playing. The Agha's house was old. Above the front door was a mosaic with Arabic script on it. The colonel took his glasses from his pocket and stepped out of the car. He put the glasses on and read the verse of the mosaic, "Nasr-e-man Allah va Fath-e Ghareeb—With God's Aid Rapid Victory Is Close." It was cold. He returned to the car. They were late and he was worried that the Agha's wife might have insulted his wife who was now begging for forgiveness and demeaning herself. He honked. Nothing. He turned on the car radio. The voice of the man singing about stars and acacias bored him. He thought to himself, "What nerve, to sing with a voice like that."

They finally turned up. They weren't carrying the bowl. The colonel sighed in relief. Keyvan sat next to him and said, "Grandpa, send me to an Islamic school too. I played with Mohsen, the man's son. He said they keep telling him in school that 'Your progenitors must be pleased with you.' What does 'progenitor' mean?"

"It means mother and father," replied the colonel impatiently. "But your mother has gone off to Germany to learn hairdressing, and your father has taken another wife, so you don't have parents."

"Don't talk to the child like that," retorted Mansoureh Khanoum. She turned toward Keyvan and said, "Keyvan, for the time being, we are your parents."

"Then send me to Islamic school so you, too, can be pleased with me," said Keyvan.

Snow, snow, snow. Snow was everywhere; God had whitened the face of everything in existence. The trees, the gabled roofs, television antennas, clotheslines, the greenhouse, over the pool, the flower bed, the cement bricks paving the yard—all were covered with a blanket of snow, sometimes thin and sometimes thick, but immobile. Creatures—whether standing, sitting, or lying down—seemed not to be breathing, but waiting. The world of the colonel's house had become a monstrous cat stalking a mouse.

Keyvan caught a cold. Mansoureh Khanoum had placed dried camomile flowers into a water bowl over the stove. The vapor filled the room with an air of tranquility. The colonel sat above the bed and took Keyvan's hand; it was hot. "Keyvan, my son, you'll soon be well again," said the colonel. "When the weather turns warm I'll buy you a couple of pigeons, a male and a female. And I promise not to cut their wings."

Keyvan said, "Grandpa, I told you not to cut the pigeon's wings. I knew it would hurt."

Mansoureh Khanoum came into the room and said "Dear, get up and drive to Tajrish and buy the child some turnips, vegetables for soup, and some sweet lemons."

"Where do you expect me to park the car, woman?"

"Well, then put on your boots and walk."

"Grandpa," Keyvan said, "I don't like turnip soup."

The colonel wasn't able to find sweet lemons, but he bought the turnips and the vegetables. The car slipped and slid over the ice, veering right and left. "What's the matter with the damn car?" wondered the colonel. "It even has snow tires . . ." As he turned onto Asadi Avenue, the car made a complete half-turn. Near the water fountain he caught sight of the Agha's cloak spread out over the snow. The brazier was tipped over, the coals burnt out. Farther up he saw the Agha's *shab-kolah*. Even farther, he noticed a battle going on. He stopped suddenly. The snow piled up had made it impossible to park on either side of the alley. All the same, he stepped out of his car, his shoes sinking into the snow. Two men, holding the Agha between them, were dragging him away. Haji Ali and Mr. Avakh were struggling to free him. The men, although in civilian clothes, seemed quite strong and quick, and the colonel had no doubt they were carrying guns under their jackets. They were hitting in turns the Agha, Haji Ali, and Mr. Avakh. A few men and a couple of kids turned up from the back alleys. The colonel approached stiffly and yelled out, "Wait. Hold on, this is Colonel Aryanifar!"

Everyone stopped. But the two men didn't release the Agha. The colonel came closer and turned to the two men. "What do you think you're doing? What business do you have with the Agha?"

And all of a sudden it slipped out: "Aren't you Moslems?"

The man clutching the Agha's right wrist said, "I warned him a hundred times not to sit across from the mosque. He had no ears for hearing."

"Is it a crime to sit across from the mosque?" said the colonel in anger.

"It is against the public order," replied the man. "The Doctor has declared it."

"Give the Doctor a message from me," said the colonel. "Tell him Colonel Aryanifar sends his regards and says, 'A street is a pathway for the people. Whoever pleases may sit there.' "

Suddenly he regretted what he had just said and fear took hold of him. He said to himself, "My good man, where do you suppose they'll take *you*?" He swallowed and said aloud, "Tell him that the colonel said, 'I'll call him myself . . .' "

The eyes of Haji Ali and Mr. Avakh were filled with gratitude and compassion. The Agha's eyes were perplexed.

He had to take a risk. Whatever would be, would be.

There weren't many years left for him or for his wife. His wife had longed for it; it was she who insisted, time and again, that one should be either a true Moslem or no Moslem at all. So what if they cut off his pension . . .

"Tell him for me, not to harass honest people so much," he said paternally. "You'll only reap what you sow."

He had gotten going now and was surprised that he could not stop himself. Taking the Agha's hand, he said, "Agha, sir, please take a seat in the car."

The man let go of the Agha, but he still seemed uncertain. It was the colonel now who was dragging the Agha.

"You'll catch pneumonia," said the colonel softly.

The Agha climbed into the car. Haji Ali brought his cloak, threw it around his shoulders, and put the *shab-kolah* over his head. The colonel started the car and turned on the heater. The armed men were talking together. One of them came to the car and asked, "What did you say your name was?"

"Colonel Aryanifar."

The colonel stepped on the gas pedal, and the car pulled away from the snow. "We'll go to my house," he told the Agha. "You'll have a warm cup of tea. My wife is a follower of yours."

The colonel was in bliss. Laughing, he said, "Excuse me, I forgot to greet you."

The Agha said, "Asalam Allay kom va Rahmatollah va Barakato—Peace be upon thee, and the mercy of God and his blessing."

Bronze mirror with mother and child handle
Iran, Luristan—7th century, B.C.

To Whom Can I Say Hello?

Is there really anybody left to whom I can say hello? The school headmistress is dead, Haj Ismail is lost, my one and only daughter now belongs to that wolf of a husband. The cat died, the brazier tongs fell on the spider—it died, too—and how badly it's snowing now. Every time it snows I feel so depressed I could crush my head against the wall. The doctor said, 'Whenever you feel that way get out of the house.' He said, "Whenever you feel lonely and have no one to confide in, speak out, aloud to yourself; in other words, become my own patient stone. He said, 'Go out to the fields and scream your head off. Curse whomever you wish . . .' What a snow! At first the flakes clung to each other and then separated; now it's snowing in tiny flakes. Sometimes it seems it hasn't stopped snowing since the beginning of winter."

The old snow was frozen on the ground, and people only added to it by shoveling off their roofs onto the alleys and the streets. The only ones who could now walk on those pavements were the young athletes or the children whose schools had closed because of the storm. Without snow there were high prices, shortages and talk of rationing water and electricity; with snow, the schools and life itself came to a halt.

Last night the lights had gone out along Alai Avenue, and Kokab Soltan had remained seated under her *korsy*, staring into the darkness until she went almost crazy with anxiety. She had thought if she did not leave the room and the darkness engulfing it, she would go completely mad. She had stood up, and fumbling in the dark she had gone downstairs and stood by the gate. The freezing wind blew fiercely, and she heard the cry of the neighbor's child. The night before last their water pipe had burst, and it had been three days since the garbage man had collected their trash.

Kokab Soltan, a retired employee of the Ministry of Education, did not, however, have that much trash for anyone to collect. The bursting of the pipe had not damaged any of her belongings. Her room was on the second floor next to Mr. Cheesepour's quarters—which consisted of two large rooms, a kitchen, and a bathroom. Mr. Cheesepour had three daughters all waiting to be married, and an enormous wife. The neighbors had nicknamed him Mr. Cheesepour because he owned a dairy shop on Jaleh Street and never sold anything on credit, no exceptions. His real name, though, was Mr. Shariatpour-e Yazdani.

Kokab Soltan used the downstairs kitchen only to get water for her ablutions and toiletry needs; she did not have much cooking to do, especially since her bad dentures pained her gums and made it difficult to eat. Her room was no larger than a matchbox, and she did not have much furniture. She had sent off whatever she owned to her son-in-law's house as her daughter's dowry.

Kokab Soltan got out from under the *korsy*, stood by the window and watched the snowfall. She felt nostalgic as she had been thinking about Haj Ismail for the past two nights.

"What fun we had together; pity it didn't last long. The headmistress would leave for Evin Darakeh resort in the summers. Haj Ismail would warm up the bath and wash me as clean as he could, scrubbing me, tickling me. We laughed wholeheartedly as we sweet-talked each other and read poetry to one another.

"We'd spread the carpet on the headmistress's bed in the middle of the garden and together smoke opium and slowly sip vodka until we were totally high. We'd go under the mistress's mosquito net and sleep nude in each other's arms. He taught me how to read and write. I'd read him the Amir Arsalan epic. We'd read the various epics and legends several times. The mistress had many books which we borrowed and then returned to their proper places. Haj Ismail was the school janitor, and I worked in the headmistress's house. The poor woman didn't have much work for me. I'd seed pomegranates for her and take them to school at ten o'clock. When pomegranates weren't in season, I'd take her a sherbet. I cooked only her lunch. She never had dinner—only a glass of milk before she went to bed. My God, he and I did everything we could in this town; we went to every playhouse, every movie theater. We saw *The Thief of Baghdad*, *The Arab Hanessa*, *New York's*

Secret, Arshin Malalan four or five times each. Our money was blessed, we had plenty to spend. The mistress paid me, and Haj Ismail received his salary from the Ministry."

The doctor had said, "Talk to yourself, pour out whatever makes you happy or sad. Don't keep it in . . ."

"We went to Karbala to pray. We repented and asked Imam Hossein to grant us a child. The Lord gave us Robabeh. It was the next year that Haj Ismail went to work one morning and never returned. The headmistress, the secret police, the police department, everyone looked for him. Even I would take Robabeh in my arms everyday and go from one office to another asking about him, but it was as if Haj Ismail had never existed. He had disappeared.

"I used to put Robabeh to sleep and sit by myself and smoke opium. I addicted the mistress's cat. As soon as the smell of opium rose, it would come sit next to me, close its eyes, and purr away. I blew the smoke toward the cat, and it would stretch its body. The cat died a natural death. Next I addicted the spider. It had spun a web in the corner of the room. As the smell of opium reached it, it would climb down and not budge from beside the brazier. The tongs fell on it. The spider died, too.

"The headmistress filled out an application and employed me as janitress, filling Haj Ismail's place, and kept me in her house until the day she died. God bless her soul. She used to say, 'You now have twice as much work to do, but so much the better. The only way to tolerate this long life without a friend is through hard work.' She was upset about my smoking opium and nagged at me until I gave it up. Besides I had so much work to do that I rarely had time to smoke. In the house I took care of the mistress's affairs; in school I did the cleaning, washed the benches, delivered the girls' report cards to their homes, and received tips. Around "New Year's"[24] I planted nasturtium bulbs, wheat, and lentils in clay pots and placed them in the mistress's room, or took them to the teachers' houses. I would get tips ranging from two to ten *tomans*. I did all the work so Robabeh could have a happy and comfortable life. I dressed her up like the daughters of the wealthy, until she received her high school diploma. Had the headmistress not died, I would never have given her away in marriage. The mistress died, and I became homeless. They retired me after eighteen years of work. They said, 'Your time has come,' and they kicked me out of the mistress's house. I was forced to ruin my child's future and marry her off to that bloody bastard; the jerk works in Mr. Lachini's notary office. What else could I have done? The girl was quite pretty, dressed like the rich, went to the hairdresser every week. How was I going to afford such a lifestyle in a rented room with a measly pension? And besides, she hadn't been accepted at the university.

"The doctor said to curse loudly whomever I want, to get it off my chest. And so cursing has become my prayer language. God only knows, I used to be a carefree person; I loved streams, greenery, and the moon in the sky. No one had ever taught me to fast and pray all the time. When we went to Karbala, I did the prayers standing behind Haj Ismail; he said all the prayers out loud and I would repeat them silently to myself. When we returned to Tehran, I forgot them all. Instead, I know how to curse. I curse all

---

[24]The Persian New Year is March 21, the first day of Spring.

cowards of all time. I curse all the men who have lost their honor and have become detestable cowards. Many, though, remained honorable; stood up for what they believed and died for it. Many just got lost and disappeared. May the Lord rest the souls of everyone's dead. The headmistress used to say, 'Our misfortune is that we turn our men into cowards.' She'd say they suck our blood through pipelines and leave us, bloodless and cowards.

"They brought Mirza Reza Kermani, the murderer of Nasseredin Shah Qajar, into the audience hall where the aristocrats, the wealthy, and the pillars of the government sat around and kept saying, 'Mirza Reza, say hello.' He kept asking: 'To whom should I say hello?'

"The headmistress would say: 'His grandmother had gone to Ayn o-Dowleh, the prime minister, taken off her head scarf, put it on his head and tied it under his chin . . .' I wish to go and buy all the cloth in the shops, make them into scarves and tie them around every single coward's head. All the light that pours on your grave isn't enough, head Mistress. You were right; women have a hundred times the honor of . . .

"I should go buy milk to make rice pudding. No, I'll make some *fereni*.[25] But how can I go with all this ice? The American boots I recently bought are too large for me and give me blisters; my neck and my right ear are screaming with pain, my right knee is aching, and since last night, I haven't been able to stop thinking about Haj Ismail. My head is pounding. Nevertheless, I must go, because if I sit

---

[25]*Fereni*: pudding made with ground rice, milk, and sugar, usually for babies who still have not teethed.

alone in this room and keep talking to myself, I shall go crazy. Once again my stomach is churning with anxiety. I will wrap newspapers around my feet and put the woolen socks I knitted myself over the newspapers; then the boots will fit fine. Being able to knit has been quite a blessing these days; it makes me forget about thinking and imagining things. I must have knitted at least ten sweaters for Mansour and Mas'ud. I knitted such lovely patterns, but their father has forbidden them to accept presents from me. Now I keep knitting and unraveling. I have no one to knit for, nor do I have the extra money to waste with this inflation, which has raised all prices. The only thing which comes cheap these days is human life.

"That very first day I told him I had only this child in the entire world; it would be a crime to separate me from my one and only child. That jerk, though, despised me from the very beginning, otherwise why did he move to the Saba Garden area? It was just to spite me, and then when I spoke my mind—which happened to be the truth—he took my hand and threw me out of my child's house. I know what to do. I'll go and learn the infamy prayers from Mrs. Cheesepour. I'll wear my pants over my head and do the infamy prayers over the toilet roof to spite my bloody son-in-law. I will put a curse on him. Mrs. Cheesepour knows all kinds of prayers—wasn't she the one who told me, on the roof the other day, to do the infamy prayers? On Thursday nights they listen to Mr. Rashed's sermon on the radio and turn the volume high so that all the neighbors can hear. I wished I could listen to the songs of Ghamar ol-Moluk Vaziri, who sang so beautifully. The headmistress had a few of her records; I

don't know who got hold of them. Summers she'd go to
Evin Darakeh, God bless her soul, and the school was
closed. We watered the garden thoroughly, especially the
petunias, which we had planted ourselves. We would then
sit under the vine trellis, wind the record player, and listen
to Ghamar ol-Moluk or Zelli, or Eghbal ol-Sultan. I would
make lemon quince sherbet and bring it to Haj Ismail, who
would refuse, saying, 'You drink first . . .' If only Robabeh
would come for a short while and bring Mansour and
Mas'ud along with her, how much better I'd feel. I once
told Mas'ud, 'You're so cute I could eat you up.' He turned
around and snapped, 'Eat yourself up.' I begged him to let
me kiss him, he said 'Buy me some bubble gum first,' I said,
'No gum.' The headmistress never liked children chewing
gum. She said it was an American habit. The infamy
prayers must be said on the roof of the toilet after sunrise.
After that you have to curse Mo'avieh and Yazid.[26] Mrs.
Cheesepour told me all about it. Before winter she had
come to the roof to wash and prepare some herbs. The
sunshine felt good, and I had gone up there to hang my
wash to dry. I felt so depressed and lonely that I went up
to her and said hello. That day we talked to each other
about all sorts of things. I told her that I had had all the
happiness in the world and had done whatever there was
to do. Then I told her about my son-in-law and how
miserable he had made me. She told me to do the infamy
prayers and the Lord would dishonor him. From that day

---

[26]Mo'avieh and Yazid were father and son, Umayyad Caliphs. Mo'avieh fought against
Ali, the prophet Mohammad's son-in-law, and Yazid fought against Ali's son Hossein, who was killed at the Battle of Karbala. This made Hossein a martyr and made
permanent a division in Islam between the party of Ali (Shi'i) and the majority Sunni.

on, I don't know why, she never spoke to me again. Every time we saw each other, she pretended she had never set eyes on me before in her life. I didn't say hello to her anymore either. All the same, I shall go and ask her about the infamy prayers. I wish it were sunny and the toilet roof wasn't covered with so much snow. God has shaken his torn quilt; cotton has poured everywhere and it's still coming down. God forbid, I think I'm totally crazy. I'll never learn my lesson. Woman, it's because you've cursed so much that all this trouble has come down on your head.

"The only thing I ever said to him was, 'How can you call yourself a man? You and your good-for-nothing brothers are killing my daughter. She's nine months pregnant, takes the boy to school, holding his lunch box in one hand and his, your bastard's son's, arm in the other. She washes all your clothes, irons, cooks lunch and dinner. All your mother ever does is to play with her prayer beads and order her around, and your brothers act as if they've been sent a maid. Even you, when you get back from the office you're dead beat; my child has to wash your feet with warm water and scrub your corns. I have seen it with my own two eyes . . .

"When I went to their house, a little depressed, I'd come back with a hundred times more sorrow. He would be nasty, his mother would constantly put me and my daughter down, and his brothers mocked me; I felt like dying. I rarely went there. One afternoon I went to Mas'ud's kindergarten to see him. I saw Robabeh holding his arm in one hand and his lunch box and the grocery bag in the other. The pregnant woman kept slipping on the ice, and Mas'ud kept nagging her to carry him in her arms as well. I picked him up and walked with my daughter to their ugly house. He was sitting under the *korsy* carelessly cracking seeds. His bloody mother was doing her prayers in the corner of the room; his brothers were not home yet. I said, 'Do you call yourself a man?' I opened up and cursed him as much as I could. He was stupefied, got out from under the *korsy*, took my hand, dragged me to the door and threw me out of the house. He called me a wicked witch, a shrew, a despicable monster, and other horrible things . . .

"Besides, he also beats my poor daughter, I've heard it from the neighbors. I've heard he's told her, 'Hasn't your mother raised you from the money she's earned as a housekeeper and janitor?' I've even heard that my daughter had to deliver Mansour without a midwife. He must be twenty months old now, probably speaking too. I've heard his mother said, 'Why does she need a midwife for her second pregnancy?' So she delivered the baby herself. The neighbors helped as well. When I heard these stories, I couldn't take it anymore. I went out and bought three kilos of tangerines and went to visit my daughter. Her pallor was yellow like turmeric. Oh how sick she looked, she hardly had the strength to move around in her bed. She begged me to leave, to go and take the tangerines as well, saying, 'If he finds out you've come here he'll beat me up so bad God knows when I'll get out of bed.' I noticed the dirty clothes heaped up in the corner; I lost my temper and said, 'Robabeh, may your mother die for you, this is no life, this is death. Your father and I enjoyed life to its fullest, why should you waste away like this? How many times do you think you'll get the chance to live? Your father used to change your diapers, sing you lullabies, wash you, take you out for walks.' She said, 'Mother I have two children, how can I get a divorce? Besides, he's not nasty to *me*.' I said, 'If all you wanted was to be a maid, you'd not have had to study the way you did.'

"Oh, Robabeh, who are you kidding? What else did you want him to do to you? He's forbidden me to go to Mas'ud's school. I have to go to the butchers, the grocery store, and the dairy shops near my daughter's house so that perhaps I'll see one of their neighbors; they probably see her or hear that bastard's voice. I've heard that Robabeh has to wear glasses now, most likely because she studied so much, or perhaps he's hit her on the side of the head and she's lost her vision. What horrible things I hear; I hear that he's hit Mas'ud and blood's come out of his ear, I hear . . . I curse him so much that if one of my curses comes to be he'll be done in forever; but, alas, tyrants always remain unharmed.

"Oh, Robabeh, your father and I had all the fun in the world. I never denied you anything, I promised not to let you work as long as you lived in my house, thinking you would do your share when you got married and left for your husband's home. But I never imagined you'd have to toil this hard. His ungrateful sisters come and stay at their dear mother's house as soon as they're ill. May they go to hell with their 'mother dear.' Who nurses you when you're sick? Robabeh, of course. 'Robabeh hurry up and bring fruit juice, hurry up and cook chicken soup, hurry up and go buy milk and warm it up for us.' The headmistress, God bless her soul, used to say, 'You don't let this child lift a finger. You're making sure she only spends her time studying. You're trying to take her out of her social class,

but you don't realize that women, in reality, belong to the
working class.' May light pour over your grave, woman,
how knowledgeable you were.

"I should go buy some milk and make rice pudding. No,
I'll make *fereni*. These bloody dentures are really bothering
me. The doctor said, every time your loneliness starts to
get to you, get up and go out . . ."

She stood and looked in the mirror. Her hair was white
at the roots, then it gradually became red, and the tips
were jet black. No wonder her son-in-law had called her a
wicked witch. What he did not know, though, was that
white hair grows out of a sorrowful heart. When she was
pregnant with Robabeh, in her final months, her heart
would itch. The headmistress would say, "The child is
growing hair." She used to say that the child's hair takes
root at the mother's heart. She would say, "No matter how
we look at it, the way it stands today, women belong to the
working class."

She lifted the corner of the *korsy* and took out one *toman*
from under the mat. What a pity she had sent those two
Kurdish carpets to her son-in-law for her daughter's dowry.
She put on her veil, took her maroon umbrella and walked
out of the yard gate. She walked with care, holding on to
the wall and drainpipes and windowpanes of people's
houses. She wished she had taken her dentures out, but she
didn't want to go in front of people without them because
of all the wrinkles their absence made on her face. She had
to go down all of Alai Avenue, then behind the Plan
Organization building. Shah Abad Avenue was full of all
sorts of stores. She could go to Jaleh Street from besides
the police station and buy the milk from Mr. Cheesepour's

dairy shop. But no such luck.

The milk was finished; bottled milk, carton milk, and even the regular milk were gone, "Tehran, what good are you, with your cold, hard winters and hot, dry summers, with no rivers, trees, or streams? May you fall into ruins and collapse on top of all your cowardly, despicable and impotent inhabitants. As the headmistress used to say, it's like a dried ink spot spread out on a piece of paper. It has run everywhere, stretching its arms to all sides like a crab. May you be forever destroyed, horrible-looking, crab-like city."

She went to the butcher shop. Mr. Cheesepour's wife was buying meat. She had ordered a leg of lamb. Jafar Agha was cutting it into pieces; with his ax he was splitting the bone in half. It was good old Iranian lamb with a beautiful color—not the frozen stuff. He said, "Two kilos and seven hundred grams." Kokab Soltan thought to herself, "Well, it's not for nothing that people grow so huge and develop double chins." Mrs. Cheesepour was wearing a woolen scarf over her hair, had gloves on, and a fur coat over her suit. She took out a fifty-*toman* note from her pocket and handed it to Jafar Agha. Jafar Agha's hand was cut, and the piece of cloth he'd tied over it was stained with blood.

She waited until Mrs. Cheesepour had left. She stretched her hand and offered the one *toman* to Jafar Agha. He took some fat and skin and a tiny bit of meat and a frozen piece of bone from the counter and threw them on the scale. Kokab Soltan said, "Jafar Agha, don't give *me* the frozen meat from God knows what cemetery. It's only good for fertilizing the trees." Jafar Agha snapped, "Take it or leave

it. What did you expect to get with one *toman*, a steak?"
He put the junk meat in a piece of newspaper and handed
it to Kokab Soltan. Would he have dared insult her like
that had Haj Ismail been alive?

Kokab Soltan was overcome with fear, this fear was a
kind of disease itself. She was afraid she would remain this
lonely for the rest of her life, that her son-in-law would
never make up with her, and she would never see her
daughter again. She slipped on the ice as she came near the
gas station and almost fell down. The pavement was like
glass, and now the snow was covering the ice. Snow was
her other fear. She was afraid that it would snow so much
that she would be unable to leave her house, unable to go
to the Saba Garden district where her daughter lived.
Unable to hang around the dairy, grocery and butcher
shops, and to find out some sort of news about her child.
She was afraid that it would snow for so long that doors
could not be opened and people would have to walk on the
roofs. All her neighbors had gable roofs, therefore, she
would be the only one confined to her room like a prisoner
and would then contract the virus that everyone said had
come from Japan. She would vomit until her body became
dehydrated and then slowly would disintegrate, alone in
her room, without anyone to take care of her. She would
die and her body would decompose. But she was not afraid
of death. How could a carefree person fear death? She was
afraid of snow, disease, loneliness, closed doors, and her
son-in-law's rage, but not of death—as long as it was a
painless death and she was not aware that she was dying.
If only she could sleep and never wake up. Unlike Mrs.
Cheesepour, she was not afraid of the angels of death, the

first night of the grave, or the day of fifty thousand years. She did not believe in any of those superstitions.

Somehow, she had to occupy herself so that she would not be frightened of loneliness. How much could she knit and unknit again? She had even thought of making a patchwork quilt. She could look in her various bundles and gather whatever remainders she could find and sew a quilt with them. But for whom? After all, for whom and for what was she alive? To whom could she say hello? Who was left for anyone to say hello to?

She wondered where the kids had come from to swarm the streets, play with the snow, slide over the ice, making it more slippery for pedestrians. A snowball hit her umbrella, making a loud noise; she closed it and turned to yell at them. Had she not once been young herself? Did she not enjoy all that was fun in life? Had she done less mischief? At the beginning of Alai Avenue, the kids had built a huge snowman; it had one eye with a round black patch tied over its other eye and a black cap over its head. It seemed as if they were letting out their frustrations as they attacked the snowman they had made, with snowballs. Blood had rushed to their cheeks from the exertion of so much energy. Their eyes gleamed. One kid, slip-sliding, came toward Kokab Soltan. She had reached the drainpipe of a house close to her's. The boy kept coming closer and closer, then he suddenly slipped and hit Kokab Soltan, and they were both sprawled on the ground, but the boy quickly got up and ran away. Kokab Soltan lay on the ground, her umbrella thrown to one side and herself to the other. The meat she had bought—not meat, junk—the junk meat had fallen from her hand and was scattered all over the ice and snow. Kokab Soltan couldn't believe she could get knocked down in this way; it was as if she had been left alone, sprawled out in a forsaken desert of ice and snow. Following the doctor's instructions she began to holler, screaming, "Prissy faggot bastards. Have they closed the schools so you can kill everyone? God only knows in which cemetery you were conceived and brought up. Hey, people, help me! This unholy bastard's killed me; he threw me down and ran away. I've probably broken an arm or a leg. One of you come and help me get up. Looking la-di-da, taking fifty-*toman* bills out of your pockets, buying meat by the kilo? Is that all you know how to do? Have you ever thought of offering just a bowl of yogurt to your neighbor? May I hear the news of your death, you bloody bastard who's separated me from my child. You, Robabeh, where on earth are you to see how contemptible your mother's become? Haj Ismail, where are you? I used to be all smiles, all happiness—look at me now. I pray to God no loved one ever becomes contemptible. You mischievous kids, should one ever utter something harsh to you, all of a sudden your parents and relatives spring up from everywhere to defend you. Where are those parents and relatives now?"

A few passers-by came toward her. A young man with a black beard and glasses bent down and took Kokab Soltan's hand and helped her up from the ground. He picked up her veil, cleaned the snow off it, and placed it over her head. A good-looking veil-less lady picked up the junk meat and put it back in the newspaper and handed it to her. The young man picked up her umbrella and held it over her head; he took her arm and said, "I'll take you home." The pretty lady said, "If you think you've broken anything, we'll take you to a clinic." Kokab Soltan's heart beat fast and her mouth was bitter, nevertheless she smiled at the lady. All of a sudden, she thought of this young man as the son-in-law she wished she had, but did not, and this woman as her own daughter. Then she imagined that the entire population of the city were her relatives. For a moment her heart was warmed with this thought. She said hello to everyone, and then suddenly she began to cry. She cried as if it were only yesterday that Haj Ismail had disappeared.

Simin Daneshvar and her husband, Jalal Al-e Ahmad.

The Loss of Jalal

He died graciously, the same way he had lived. He died hastily, like the burning out of a light and in the company of those ordinary people whom he loved and whose cause he supported. I was beside him and so was Mahin Tavakoli,[27] who regarded him as her older brother. And now I understand why in all our years together he was always in a rush. He knew that time was running out; so, he was in a rush to read, learn, and try out and to experience, create and record. He wished to drink fully from the cup of every moment and then welcome all those moments with an open mind. He assessed his surroundings with intelligence, curiosity and contemplation, and never

---

[27]Mahin Tavakoli is the wife of Mirza Abol-Ghasem Tavakoli; they were two of our best friends. Jalal had dedicated *In Support and Betrayal of Intellectuals* to this couple.

allowed them to become tarnished, because he meticulously dusted and honed them to shine like a mirror.

Jalal knew his path and walked it with compassion. He never calculated; he had an intrinsic nobility, and if he turned to religion, it was because of knowledge and insight. He had already experimented with Marxism, socialism, and to some extent, existentialism. And his relative return to religion and the belief in the coming of the Mahdi[28] was a way toward freedom from imperialism and the assertion of a national identity. It was a way of achieving human dignity, compassion, justice, logic, and virtue. This was the kind of religion Jalal wanted. From the Constitution onward, the Imperialists' viewpoint was that freedom for us meant freedom for them to exploit and export our oil and other resources to the West. Jalal, however, opposed precisely this kind of freedom. For him, freedom was deliverance from Russian Stalinist Marxism and English and American imperialism. It was for this reason that he tried to unravel the visible and invisible threads in his work. Perhaps this was the cause of his death, or at least his deep frustration leading to his premature death. Jalal had the courage to spit in the face of the exploiters and the colonialists; he dared to attack the intellectuals for the benefit of the people and for their own sake. But Jalal never wanted power. He wanted influence—of which he had plenty over his contemporaries, and it was predicted that he would have it over later generations as well. There were many who could be bought with money or status or women

---

[28]Mahdi: Arabic, meaning divinely guided one. In Islamic eschatology, a messianic deliverer who will fill the Earth with justice and equity, restore true religion, and usher in a short golden age lasting seven, eight, or nine years before the end of the world.

or drugs, and in our time the number of people for sale were not few. Jalal, on the other hand, this proud mullah's son, had gone through and experienced the progressive stages of intellectual development step by step. He depended on his strong and courageous personality and could not be fooled. He never lapsed, never gave in. Nevertheless, at no time did he pretend to be a genius, and I have never intended to make an idol out of him. Idol-making, which is one of the specialties of our people, is not particularly to the advantage of the idol they create, and in the final analysis, it works against the people themselves. I have never created a saint out of Jalal; he was an honest and devoted writer and a disciplined man, to the extreme of sacrificing himself.

Many times I have wanted to write about the ending of Jalal's life, but I have been unable to. And even now I know that I will not be able to create a piece of writing worthy of him, mainly because the pain still lingers. Once I began like this: "And now I shall fill the eyes with tears by telling the story of Jalal Al-e Ahmad, although I am no historian like Beyhaghi but neither was Jalal a hero like Hassanak-e Vazir—nor did he ever want to be."

On Wednesday morning, the tenth of September, 1969, he placed his finger above his clavicle—where the jugular vein beats—and said: "It hurts, it hurts badly." Tuesday at sundown he had gone swimming in the sea, even though the sea had not been at its best and the weather was cloudy. We had seen flocks of migrating birds returning from the northwest, and knew that their return was a sign of the coming cold season. He put on his work clothes and started to fix our heater, which had smoked when he had tested it one rainy day. He had designed the heater and our two rooms on the Caspian Seashore himself. He had built the heater himself. He had also built the heater in Mohandess[29] Tavakoli's house. He had become an expert in fixing heaters, and until then he had either designed or built a total of eleven heaters for his friends, in addition to repairing their stoves every time they broke down. Nezam, our so-called housekeeper, hung around bringing him mortar and bricks; I was placing the groceries I had bought in the cabinets. Once in a while, I would place a cigarette in a holder and put it to his lips and strike a match for him. Both his hands were occupied; he was wearing my plastic gloves, which I used when I dyed my hair, and had torn them in several places, as they were too small for him. I was putting the food supplies in the cabinets because he wanted to return the following week with Sa'edi; that was why he was fixing the heater. He wanted to come back with Dr. Sa'edi and go to Heru Abad to study Tatti, the native dialect.

He knew that once again he "would be made unemployed," which meant they would take away his teaching job at the Narmak Technical School. It wasn't the first time for him; he had become used to being laid off. Previously he had been excused from the Teachers College, the Mamazan Teachers College, the College of Education — each time after three, two, and one year, respectively. No extraordinary event had occurred this time that the Narmak Technical School should not follow suit.

He finished work around noon and went to take a bath.

---

[29]Mohandess: title for an engineer.

As usual, I went and washed his back with soap. He asked if he should shave his beard—he had let it grow. It is amazing how a forty-six-year-old's hair and beard could turn almost completely white. I said:

"No, Jalal, don't shave your beard, it looks very good; and besides, you're planning to come back here."

Friday, Mohandess Tavakoli and other friends were supposed to come to our place, and we were all to go back to Tehran together. He had called his mother and promised her to be back by Friday and end her patient waiting.

He came up to the top room; I was packing the suitcase. Sitting behind his desk, he said: "Pity, this one isn't finished." He was referring to his *European Travel Notes*. Since the fifth of Tir,[30] when we had come to Asalem, he had been working on his Russian, American, Israeli, and European travel notes every day from 8:30 to 11:30 A.M. He intended to publish all four together and sarcastically call it *The Four Kaabas*. After he finished his work, he would go for a swim; later in the afternoon, after an hour's rest, he would busy himself with planting flowers, painting benches, chopping firewood, and things like that. Most afternoons we either had guests or people who had come to the seashore to go swimming. Often a few SAVAK agents would also show up; it took us a while to recognize who they were, but Jalal, nevertheless, always spoke his mind. In the evenings, we would take a walk along the shore, barefoot.

Jalal said, "I'll take you back on Friday. I had a good time; how about you?" I had also had a good time.

---

[30]Tir: Persian month, equivalent to 22 June to 22 July.

We had *ghormeh sabzi*[31] for lunch. Dr. Taqizadeh's wife had brought us the vegetables from Rasht on Monday as a gift. She had bid us farewell and we knew that they were leaving on vacation. Dr. Taqizadeh was the lumber mill's doctor, and we also imposed on him. Where we lived, a gift of fresh vegetables was highly regarded, as they were extremely rare. Jalal had purchased all kinds of books on vegetable gardening, poultry, and trees so that next year he could start a real garden. For the time being, we had a small patch in which we grew watermelon, tomato, cucumber, and corn, and Jalal was the gardener. Jalal, I believe, had been a gardener all his life. He had been the gardener of his readers and his students, whom he watched in the same way he watched a tree grow and gain strength. He was a gardener to whomever he saw and thought may have a hidden talent waiting to be nurtured. He would make the talent known to the person, and then he tended and cared for it until it would bloom. He had also bought, in the town of Hashtpar, a book on cultivating roses. He did not know that he himself was the genuine flower, like his life which was a constant blossom, at least that is the way it was for me. His mother told me on the day he was buried: "Child, don't cry; the Lord is a flower picker."

We usually went to Hashtpar for shopping, and sometimes we would stop at the lumberyard in Asalem. Hashtpar, the center of Tavalesh, was almost sixteen kilometers away. A narrow winding road four kilometers long, through ricefields, connected the seashore to the main

---

[31]*Ghormeh sabzi*: an Iranian dish with green vegetables and meat cooked like a stew and eaten over rice.

road. Behind the fields was the forest of mostly alder trees; the Russians were busy installing a gas pipe in that area. We used to see them once in a while, either in their cars or walking; but we could not understand each other's language. In the middle of the forest, the rice growers' huts, *neparis*,[32] were scattered here and there.

One day, Jalal stopped his car next to a rice paddy, took his notebook and pencil from his pocket, and started to write. I was used to this habit of his. In his car's glove compartment, in his pocket, and on his bedside table he always kept a notebook and a pencil; he wrote down whatever came to his mind or what his companions said which seemed interesting to him. That day I asked him:

"What did you write?"

"I wrote," he replied, "that the main food of the people of the Far East is rice, and that their artists' inspiration stems from the rice fields which are so smooth and soft. This is why their miniatures are so delicate and exquisite. The main food of the majority of the rest of the world's population is wheat, which is harsher than rice."

"I should have thought of that," I said, "but I had never made the connection."

He said, "Look at how playfully they bend left and right with the breeze."

The beginning of the narrow road was filled with sand which the high tide had brought in. Then there was a bridge made out of tree trunks laid next to each other and then again another bridge, which was not steady at all. As we

---

[32]*Nepari*: in the northern province of Mazandaran, a platform built on top of very long pillars used for storing crops, also used as a resting place.

turned to the right toward the northwest, a narrow gravel path connected Khalif Abad to Asalem and then to Hashtpar; whenever it rained, this narrow road became a mud path. The Mirza (Mohandess Tavakoli), as Jalal used to call him, owned the land on which we had our two rooms. It was in Khalif Abad, and the lumber mill to our southeast was also in Khalif Abad. But either for ease or for beauty, they called the factory—the factory which Mirza had raised like his own child—Asalem, and where we were was also known as Asalem . . . No, you will not find it on any map.

At lunch, Jalal wanted to have some of the Persian melon on the table in front of him, but I moved it aside. He said, "My throat isn't hurting any more!" He joked and joked and made me and Mahin laugh uncontrollably. The night before he had also really made us laugh. He didn't let us have a bad time. He thought he had taken us away from civilization, dragged us to the wilderness, and offered us nothing other than the sea and the forest, and we were lonely and bored. But whoever was with Jalal could never be lonely. Throughout the years we were together, I grew consistently farther apart from friends and relatives and closer to him. He was enough for me. When friends and relatives lamented our childless state by saying our oven is not burning, I laughed because there is no oven that burns like my heart. At lunch the day before, he had asked Mahin and me:

"Where do you wish you could live?"

"Wherever you are," I said, and I read him this poem:

"Say, which city the best of them be?
He said, 'That city where my lover be.' "

To this day I hold the same belief, and I cannot imagine

that the time to rejoin him can be too far away. I feel every day I melt a little. Bury me in Jalal's tomb; I have taken care of the deed.

We lay down to rest that afternoon. The rain was pouring, stitching sky to earth. He got up at 3:30 P.M. and said, "I don't know why I feel cold. Make me a hot lemonade with an aspirin and two vitamin Cs," and then he left for Mahin's house where the heater was on. I took the things he had asked for and went there too. Then Keshvar, our maid, brought tea. He told her to bring him cigarettes, and she did. There were only three left in the wooden cigarette box. He said, "Go and get a whole pack." Nezam came and reported, "Sir, two people have come with a truck and are taking sand from our land." They mixed the earth with cement and made blocks, and the new buildings in the area were built predominantly with such materials. They also made openings in them for passing the electric wires and water pipes. Jalal said laughing, "I'll be right there to assert Mirza's landownership." We went back to the house together. Jalal put on his boots, took his cane, and left. When he came back, his face was terribly pale. I asked him, "Did you assert ownership?" "They were Turks," he said, "couldn't speak Persian." He took off his boots and said, "A strange pain started in my ankle and came all the way up to my chest and from one wrist to the other. Cross shaped." Now the rain fell harder, and it was 4:30 in the afternoon. Jalal said: "I worked too much; I'm quite tired. I'll go and sleep now." I handed him his pajamas; he put them on and went to bed. I gave him the book *The Moon Eagle*, which he had asked for and lit the candle next to his bed. He began to read, and I busied myself cleaning up. He said, "Wife, literature is becoming terribly 'experimental.' " Then he added "If this body doesn't let me down, there's nothing I can't do." "Jalal dear, why should it let you down?" I said. "This year you've been the healthiest ever." For some time experimental literature had interested him; but what was his own work in reality, if not experimental? The news reports on the atomic bombing of Hiroshima had become a form of literature in themselves. Jalal used to say, journalism approached literature which made him even more enthusiastic and eager. Then *Kon Tiki* by Thor Heyerdahl and *In Cold Blood* by Truman Capote were published at the same time. Gradually discovering truth and seeking reality and the willingness to endanger one's life, or hard-headed persistance gave form to pure literature. Hemingway's role in the formation of this school of writing should not be forgotten either. And Jalal, from the beginning, had done this.

Mahin had come upstairs to ask about Jalal. I told her that when he had come back from asserting ownership his face was terribly pale.

"Jalal, do you want me to massage your legs?" she asked.

Jalal said, "I can't even stand the blanket." Then he added, "You two go away until I concentrate my thoughts and figure out what sort of pain this is."

"I'm cold; if you could get me a hot-water bottle . . ."

We went to Mahin's house; we did not have a hot-water bottle. Mahin found a plastic bottle. She washed it and filled it with boiling water. She is indeed, a full-fledged lady. I took the bottle to Jalal and laid it next to his feet. I wanted to leave him alone. I came to Mahin's house. Mahin called Nezam and ordered him to kill a rooster and give it to Keshvar to make soup for the master.

"Nezam, turn the electricity on earlier," I said. "The master is reading in candlelight." The rain was still pouring, and the sound of the waves raging as they hit the shore could be heard.

We had a gasoline powered electric generator. When we turned it on we had to wait until the water tank above the well was full before turning on the lights.

"I should go get the doctor," I told Mahin.

"You can't, with this rain and these roads," she said. "Wait until the morning."

We had very little gasoline left; we had to get some for the electric pump.

I went upstairs to Jalal, who said, "That pain came back again; I called you several times, but you didn't hear me." Then he said, "The Coriban D was on the table; I took one. Find out how many aspirin we have left." I counted; we had seven.

"Well that should be enough until morning," he said.

"Jalal, dear, you can't take so many aspirin," I said. "I have to go and get the doctor."

"But Dr. Taqizadeh isn't here," he said.

"I'll go to Hashtpar and ask Dr. Nouhi to come."

"No, don't worry; it's nothing," he said. "I'm scared you'll have an accident in this rain. We'll wait until morning."

Nezam had forgotten to turn off the water switch on time, and the water had spilled over. Jalal heard the sound of the water spilling and almost yelled, "One day I'm not there to oversee . . . Ask him couldn't he have turned off the water switch on time?" I opened the window and said,

"Nezam, the master says . . ."

I turned on the light, and Jalal who had read the book without closing it, carefully and delicately—as always—put it on the table facing up and put out the candle wick with his two fingers. He said, "I can't breathe easily. Find an oil cloth and put it on my back." I searched for an oil cloth, which I couldn't find; I heard Jalal taking long breaths. Mahin had come upstairs too.

"How is Jalal?" she asked.

"Not so good," I said. "I'm going to get the doctor any way I can; it's better than sitting here and worrying."

"I sent Nezam to fetch the doctor," said Mahin. By this time Jalal was snoring heavily, and fear had overtaken my entire being.

I ran and started the car and picked up Nezam on the way. The rain poured so hard that the windshield wipers could not handle the flow. My head kept bumping against the inside roof of the car. Nezam asked, "Ma'am, the master must be very sick for you to drive this fast."

I said, "Nezam, pray; beg the Lord."

We reached the area where the mill employees lived. We knocked on the doors, begging for help. I went to Seyyed Mohamad's house—he was a loyal student of Jalal's. The poor fellow had just returned from the forest. I begged him, "I know you're exhausted and wet from the rain, but Jalal isn't well at all. Go to Hashtpar with the jeep and bring Dr. Nouhi. Bring back an ambulance and an oxygen tank." Near the clinic, a door to one of the houses was open. I went inside. It was the mill's medical assistant's house. I yelled, "Ambulance! Oxygen!" I was begging and yelling, and people had swarmed out of their homes. I told the medical assistant, "Now that you have neither an ambulance nor an oxygen tank, bring a camphor shot, the blood pressure pump . . . Coramin . . ." With the assistant and Mrs. Ghahremani, we sat in the car. Seyyed was driving ahead of us in his jeep. He was driving as if the car had grown wings. At the end of the narrow path, our car got stuck in the sand. I held the assistant's hand and ran in the dark. I went to Jalal's side, put my lips to his forehead. It was hot. I regained hope. The assistant took his blood pressure and then shook his head.

I said, "Why aren't you giving him a shot?"

"I'll wait until the doctor gets here," he replied. "His blood pressure is very low."

I looked at Jalal. I saw him staring at the window, as if his eyes were piercing through the rain and the darkness, hovering over the alder trees, in order to reach the sea. He had a smile on his lips. Calm and serene, as if he had learned the secret of everything. As if they had opened the curtain from both sides and revealed the secrets and now he was smiling. He was smiling and saying, "I fooled you all; I'm leaving now."

This was the worst thing he ever did to me in his life.

Dr. Nouhi and Seyyed Mohamad arrived. I asked, "Where's the ambulance? Where's the oxygen tank?" I was fooling myself. The doctor went to Jalal's side. When he came back, he asked me what had happened, and I explained everything in detail. Mahin handed the doctor an envelope, but he refused the money. Seyyed Mohamad insisted on taking me to his house, but how could anyone leave?

The world was crying. They gave me a shot and a

sleeping pill. But I had never been so awake in my entire life, never cried so heartily. Keshvar, Mahin, and I leaned our heads against each other and sobbed. In the blink of an eye, that remote and calm place was filled with people. We were gathered in Mahin's house. Mrs. Ghahremani was sitting beside me. She was sitting there on purpose, to remind me that a long time before me and at a younger age than I she had been widowed. She had tended her several children by herself, worked singlehandedly to earn their livelihood. Mrs. Alami had come as well; they had brought her intentionally, to remind me that when her four-year-old daughter, who we all adored, had gone to play on the swing, the board had broken and thrown her down, killing her instantly. All the lights were on except the light in my heart, and I knew that soon the gasoline would be finished and darkness would spread over the sea and the forest and the rain. When darkness fell, it was so dense it almost seemed one could squeeze it in one's hand, turning the alder trees into horrific monsters.

But it did not happen that way. They emptied their cars' gas tanks and filled the electric generator, and the lights stayed on all night. They went to Rezvan Deh and brought back a Shi'a who recited the Koran—where we lived, it was predominantly Sunni. Mr. Malekian and Mr. Karamian, who managed the Asalem lumber mill and whom Jalal regarded as true woodwork artists, stayed up all night and built him the best of all coffins from the best of their wood. They knew he had to travel a long journey and his body was soft and delicate and had no tolerance.

They set up a bed, and I lay down on it, like a stranger, one without a mate, so that perhaps the others would return to their homes and go to sleep. I had remembered the day Jalal and I had gone to Kermanshah. They had called early in the morning and, with no consideration, had given us news of the tragedy. They said that my sister Homa Daneshvar had had a heart attack. Jalal had taken the phone from me and yelled, "Sir, this is no way to relay such news to a woman!" The man was a general. Then they spoke in French and he made me go under the shower and packed my suitcase himself. In Kermanshah I noticed he had brought me black clothes as well. He had made up his mind that he would take me to Kermanshah for the last visit. He was always like that. What he had to do, he did fast. We set out. First, he took me to the College of Fine Arts and let my brother know; then to make sure, he called the newsbearer again. He also called his sister and his mother and gave some instructions. It was obvious from his instructions that we would never make it in time, and it would be too late. At sunset we reached the entrance to the town, and my sister's corpse (the mother of Laily Riahi) was being carried away in the ambulance, but we had not noticed—Jalal was driving too fast.

They took us to one of their friend's houses. Jalal advised me that "One doesn't take one's mourning to a stranger's house." As soon as we went inside, though, we both broke down and cried our hearts out. When everybody in the house had gone to sleep, Jalal went and bought candles and cigarettes and stayed up with me until morning. I thought I would never calm down; but Jalal had the talent to calm anyone down, with those greenish brown eyes and beautiful lips and teeth of his, with that voice which could caress, soothe, direct, and be sympathetic and in its proper time could roar like thunder. No one but he could endear the principles of justice so lovingly, and no one but he could become so vindictive in the face of injustice. At least I have not come across another person like him in my long years.

He said, "Wife, life slaps one in the face; when you receive the slap you will probably get dizzy and be finished; you will fall and no one will help you to your feet. You must place your hands on your knees and say 'Ali my Lord' and stand up by yourself. Sometimes you may not be able to. But from the slap of life one may also become aware; you try to become aware."

And now he himself was dead. And I had decided, as it would have pleased him, to remain conscious in the face of this great slap of time. But how was I to do it? I wished he were here and could tell me how. The only possible form of consciousness for me was to remain in his trail and carry on his way of justice. Besides, was there any other course for me to take? This was how I decided, as Azarm says, to become the patient stone of this public catastrophe.

But there was another approach to achieving awareness: to learn about death—death which grows in one's arms, so close that it seems to be sitting calmly in one's lap. Is death the pilgrimage of the eyes to distant lands? It is amazing how it dazzles the eyes and opens up lips to smiles. Will the eyes ever tire of such a sight? Is death a breaking away? Is it an infinite "no" that has completely overwhelmed the eyes with its marvel? Or is it merely a fan blowing onto the soul? You exist one instant, and the next you are gone. It does not matter how desperately they call you back, how infinitely they wish for you; it does not matter how much sleep they lose in your memory every night until dawn as they toss from side to side and how despairingly they grieve and regret your absence. What is the use of all the suffering?

Early in the morning everyone came, whoever had seen and got to know him in the last two months and the last days. The women, the men, and the children who worked in the rice fields and to whom he had often given rides, rain or shine, were all there. The men who stayed up all night beating on drums to drive away the boars from the rice fields had come as well. With their drum beating, they denied everyone their sleep, and Jalal used to take a few packs of Oshnou cigarettes and go to them. The first night he had gone, they had treated him like a stranger; later they considered him even more than a friend. Mr. Toutian came from Hashtpar with a cab. The forest engineers who had gone to Rasht for vacation came back. A large number of Asalem lumber mill workers came as well, but they had to return to work early. Seyyed Mohammad, his eyes filled with tears, consoled me like a brother. He left to get the death certificate from Dr. Nouhi. Heart attack. That is all. Seyyed Mohammad used to build pathways in the splendid forest, and Jalal had gone to see him several times in the woods. He was his favorite student in the Shahpour school in Tajrish (now the Jalal Al-e Ahmad school). Jalal had planned with Seyyed's help to gather the names of the local trees, flowers, and bushes and dry the herbs which had medical usage and record their names and families and bring onto paper the life which got lost in the commotion of the forest. We had gone to Par-e Sar forest once. The women had brought the cows to the summer quarters and had set up tents in the vast grazing grounds. They invited us to their tents, served us tea, and all the time their hands were busy knitting patterned, but rough, men's socks, which they sold for five *tomans*. Jalal bought a few pairs, which I knew would never come to any use. He then explained to them that with a softer wool and the same patterns, they could knit sweaters and cardigans and even coats. He said, "Wife, next year set up a knitting workshop. Cut models for them . . ." Which next year?

A tall straight woman was the temporary supervisor of the families, and she had several children and grandchildren of her own. Her memories were filled with all kinds of stories and sorrows. That day she had not greatly welcomed Jalal's plan. When they returned from summer camp, we saw them in Khalif Abad. The cows were walking ahead and a mule carrying the tribe's belongings followed from behind. The tall straight woman was riding another mule, and behind her was sitting, probably, her youngest grandchild. She said hello to us. We knew her name was Khanoum Gol.[33] She said she would be waiting for us next year. Khanoum Gol, too, had come. She was standing under an alder tree and crying hard and looking at me with all the sympathy in her heart. Shahrbanou, Nezam's wife, was also there. I knew she had recently given birth, her complexion resembled the color of red earth. When he heard Shahrbanou had had a baby, Jalal ordered us to pay her a visit. It was a few days before his death. A porch and a room, in one of the rice fields, and a few odds and ends were the sum total of Nezam's belongings. The woman was sitting on a torn quilt, her infant lost in the heap of things around her. She had a fire going with wood; the

---

[33]Khanoum Gol: literally means Flower Lady.

entire room was filled with smoke. The water was boiling in a smoky kettle on top of the fire. Mahin had brought the newly born a blanket, and I . . . Shahrbanou's look was just like Khanoum Gol's. It was as if they all knew they were connected to Jalal in some way—meaning Jalal was connected to them—but they did not know what kind of connection it really was. They knew they had to come, and they had; but they did not know for sure why they should have come.

I caught sight of Mohandess Mojahedi. He was leaning against a tree covering his eyes with a white handkerchief. I went to him under the rain. He did judo and karate, and had sometimes discussed the miracles of these two Far Eastern sports with Jalal. I asked him, "Can judo and karate do anything in the face of death?" His sob grew louder. When he calmed down, he said, "I wish the flowers weren't wet; I'd pick them all and pour them over Jalal's coffin."

"He planted those flowers with his own hands," I replied.

Shams, Dr. Abdol Hossein Sheikh, General Riahi (my poor sister's husband and the father of Laily, my beloved adopted daughter, Mohandess Tavakoli, and Dr. Khebrehzadeh arrived from Tehran. Mahin had let them know by telegram. When they came out of the room in which Jalal had gone to his eternal sleep, I saw them. Mirza Tavakoli was standing above the stairs, his hands to his waist with eyes red and bulging out of their sockets, he was screaming, "Simin, this is impossible!" Shams could not speak, and I was saying, "One of you, think of something for this young man. Did you have to take him immediately to his brother's death bed? Didn't you know that their lives were bound together?" I thought Shams was the same young boy he was when we had gotten married. I put my arms around him and said, "Shams, I did whatever I could. What can I now say to your sisters and heartbroken mother?" Shams looked at me like a brother, compassionately. His eyes were saying, "I never reproached you." I said, "Shams, he was waiting for you; why didn't you come sooner?" Some time later, his mother would tell me, "Child, put your hand on your heart and pray for patience. Pray with me."

General Riahi had suddenly grown old and pale and was asking, "Why? Why?" He, like Jalal, was also a groom of the family and was his beloved friend and confidant. He was one of the very few who would read Jalal's writings before they were published and always offered a sound opinion. The completed edition of *Westernstruckness* was with him for the longest time.

With Dr. Abdol Hossein Sheikh, we went to Mahin's house and I described to him how it had all happened. He had already examined Jalal and detected the cause of death to be either a heart attack or an embolism. He said there was a bruise next to his jugular vein. I was seeing Dr. Sheikh's tears for the first time in my life. I said, "Sheikh, had you been here this would have never happened." I said, "I'll be indebted to you all my life. How many times have I imposed on you in the middle of the night and at all unearthly hours dragging you to Jalal's bedside. You were the one who saved him for me all these years." I said, "You are the most ingenious physician I have ever seen in my life." I still believe it and still burden him with all my own, as well as my friends', sicknesses and worries. How many patients did I send him at the beginning of the Revolution, God only knows.

General Riahi, too, joined us. He was saying, "Laily will die of grief . . ." He said, "It was Jalal who put the pen in Laily's hand and encouraged her to publish her poems in *Arash* magazine." I said, "Jalal has put pens in many hands . . ." Jalal considered Laily and her brother Ali the children he wished to have, but never did.

Dr. Khebrehzadeh convinced everyone to allow me to say my final farewell to Jalal. I neither screamed nor sobbed. I had promised. I kissed him and kissed him. In this world rarely does a woman have the fortune I had to find her perfect mate. Like two migrating birds who have found each other and become soulmates in a cage, they render their imprisonment more tolerable for each other.

They placed the coffin in the ambulance, and we set out. We stopped in front of the lumber mill. Most of the workers had come out to the street to see us off. A large number of friends came with us to the shrine of Imamzadeh Hashem. I do not know who gave the order, but the sound of the siren rose from the mill three times.

A LETTER TO THE READER

"My heart aches for your suffering and patience"

In midsummer of 1953, Prime Minister Eden of the United Kingdom together with President Eisenhower supported the conspiracy of the Shah and his twin sister and, hiring scandalous followers with a small sum of money, arranged a coup d'etat. This resulted in the fall of Mosadegh, the liberal, broad-minded and patriotic prime minister of Iran. Mosadegh's confreres of more than a century ago, like Farahani and Amir Kabir, having almost the same capacities, had a worse fate. They faced martyrdom, and Iran, with its despotic and colonial cultures, does not produce such figures often.

The verse I use as the title for my letter is from a poem by Mr. M. Omid, one of the most prominent contemporary poets of Iran, lamenting the fall of Mosadegh. This lamentation, in fact, is mourning the disasters that have befallen the Iranian nation through almost twenty-five hundred years of despotic regimes. Western exploitation started during the Renaissance, with "Humanism" being the main basis of this wonderful revolution of the West!

As an Iranian, I have suffered and I have been patient, but I endure and have great hope and faith in the future for all nations—including Iran. If only the Iranian kings had supported Farahani, Amir Kabir and Mosadegh, this hope would have been fulfilled sooner.

As an Iranian woman, I have suffered from the despotism of the regime, the exploitation of East and West, the limitations of a male-dominated culture, and a patriarchal system. But I have never lost hope.

I was the first Iranian woman who had a collection of short stories published. Although the people's response to me was my best reward, for a long time I was mostly neglected by critics, and ignored by the media which couldn't breathe without the government's consent. But still I think that the best and the last judge is the people.

Criticism in Iran is not a literary genre to be completely trusted. With some exceptions, it depends on personal relations between the critic and the criticized. If they are friends, the latter is praised; otherwise, he is abused—no matter how talented he is. The aim is—throw him out into the shade. Most critics were (and still are) among the first sex and where the talents of "the second sex" are concerned, if the personal relations (that rarely exist between men and women) extend to free relations, the "second sex" would be applauded; but I believe neither in free love nor traditional marriage. I consider the human body, as well as the soul, a holy shrine, and the one in charge of this shrine must pay homage to it.

If men and women could be friends, without sex as the only important factor of their relations, what an elevating alliance would result from their give and take as two equals! In such a case, man would not be the only active gender, nor woman the only passive one. Give and take of ideas, thoughts, mental and spiritual trends and exchange of sentiments and experiences, would result in such a deep friendship that would transcend them both. Women could tame men and lessen men's brutality with their tenderness, and men could compensate for the drawbacks of women, caused by their exploitation during so many centuries.

If such friendships were prolonged, habit and familiarity, combined with physical attractions, might welcome love, the king of kings, which enters the heart with all its glory, and then sex serves it to the peak. Ecstasy results from the union of souls and bodies.

I suppose Dr. Sigmund Freud, called the father of modern psychology, acted like a stepfather concerning Western civilization, placing so much emphasis upon sex and complexes which resulted from sexual deprivations. Apparently Dr. Freud had not tasted or experienced poverty, nakedness, rooflessness, ignorance, racial discrimination and segregation—apartheid, censorship, being watched by police constantly, being imprisoned and the phobia of being tortured and executed. Later, even some of his own followers admitted that there are complexes much stronger than those derived from sexual repressions that might form in the human subconscious, but most Western inhabitants were obsessed with sex already.

Several years ago, I visited the capital of a great ex-empire to see my niece (my adopted daughter). My ex-son-in-law wanted to entertain me to the hilt, so he took me to a private show which I left after a few minutes, thinking one would have to be impotent to enjoy such scenes. I felt sex overwhelming the life of the people. During my sightseeing, we passed many sex-shops, saw posters of many sex movies on screen and one of the television channels showed a sexy movie as a farewell programme (I don't know if that's every night or once in a while). I thought maybe that was a device to distract the minds of the younger generations from politics, especially from Communism, a phobia I felt was poisoning the blood of the authorities. Thank God, there were universities, many bookshops and libraries, museums, and galleries, concert halls and research centers; otherwise one felt that Western civilization had been put on hold.

While studying at Tehran University, I was appointed secretary of a literary club, with a male mathematics student as its president. We faced the death of Parvin E'tesami, a very prominent woman poet, and I suggested that we hold a memorial for her. I expected that since I was a woman I would be selected to talk about her or at least read several poems written by her. A poet-professor was invited to criticize her *Divan*, which he did, but in a very clever way he aroused suspicion in the audience's mind that most of Parvin's poems had been written by her father. This poet-professor happened to be one of the judges of my dissertation that was soon to be delivered. But what he did was so unfair it set fire to my heart, so that I jumped up and declared: "Sir, to write such poems as Parvin's, one would have to be a woman, one who knows cooking, sweeping . . . etc. One who has experienced pregnancy, childbirth and raising children, or at least has been a witness to such experiences. Was Parvin's father pregnant ever? Did he cook ever, or watch his wife repeat such routines everyday? Besides, Parvin's best poems were written after the death of her father. One of the best is the poem for his tombstone." No, he didn't fail me and I got my degree.

By and by, the male critics were attracted to my works and, as I read here and there, there were some comments on my short stories and novel. The most detailed one was written by Hushang Golshiri, in *Naghd-e-Aghah*. He is one of my favorite writers. Golshiri criticized my first two collections of short stories, which, as my first endeavors, were technically weak.

If Golshiri meant to throw me out into the shade, he didn't succeed. The eleventh edition of my novel was issued right after his criticism. In his article, Mr. Golshiri had promised the readers to continue to discuss my later works in the coming issue. The magazine was censored.

Thanks to Dr. Wallace Stegner, in charge of the Creative Writing Center at Stanford University (1952-1953), I learned to improve my technique by using fewer adjectives and adverbs, to make my style more powerful with nouns and verbs. He also taught me to show events instead of narrating them.

Then women writers came to my rescue, none of whom I had ever met. The first one was Mihan Bahrami, who wrote a deliberate criticism of my novel *Savushun*. It was written with such feminine compassion and understanding that Tehran Radio decided to showcase it by broadcasting it with a strong male voice, although I was considered an anti-government writer.

The second woman writer who focused the spotlight of her keen mind on me was Farzaneh Milani. Miss Milani interviewed me for several hours. Later, we both worked on the manuscript, omitting and changing parts of the interview. This was because she intended to come back home to visit her parents, and I wanted to stay home to be a witness of my own time and place, and give testimony in my writing about what kind of hot soup was being provided for us. Miss Milani's interview with me was printed in *Alephba*, a magazine published in Persian (in Paris) through the endeavors of Dr. Saedi, one of my best friends, who died in 1985. Dr. Saedi had forgotten to mention the name of the interviewer. I wrote a harsh letter to him, and in the next issue Miss Milani's name was mentioned. Letters received from abroad have informed me that Miss Milani has written an article analyzing my fiction. Also she has translated into English my last printed work: *Jalal's Sunset* [sic] and has had both printed in *Iranian Studies*. I haven't read them, but thanks to her anyway.

Now comes the third woman writer, with full hands. Miss Maryam Mafi has translated five of my stories, including "Loss of Jalal," which I wrote on the occasion of my husband's sudden death. Miss Milani had translated this earlier under the title of *Jalal's Sunset*. I have read Miss Mafi's translations and have made slight changes. Miss Mafi's English seems superb and Persian is her mother tongue, so the translations are very faithful to the original. Beyond that, she has reflected the essence and the spirit of my stories skillfully. When I read her translation of *Vakil Bazaar*, I sobbed. How well she has reflected and revealed the central symbol of the story. Passing through the Bazaar is passing through life, which delights us with different amusements, then leaves us empty handed reaching the dead end, knocking on an unknown door of a rugged house, without getting an answer. And when I read her translation of *To Whom Can I Say Hello?* I sobbed again, asking myself: Have I written all that? And how cruelly have I put the burden of my own loneliness on the shoulders of Kokab and how well has Miss Mafi revealed it!

In Iran, at the time I was writing (and I still commit this sin), if an artist, especially a writer, wanted to get famous, there were several roads in front of him or her. "Words," which are the basic elements of literature, as far as form is concerned, are more strong and less vague than "sounds" (music), than lines and colors (painting), than mud, bricks, stones (sculpture and architecture), etc. So literature was and is more watched by the government; besides it gives inspiration to other arts, including cinematography, although the latter's attractions surpass any of the other arts for the masses, whether literate or illiterate.

If a writer chose to praise the government (the Shah being its central power) by an act meant to praise the foreign power supporting him, then the whole mass media was at his or her disposal.

Our patriarchal regime and male culture, goes back to even mythological times. We can read in *The Shahnameh* by Ferdowsi that it is Rostam who kills his son. So we have the Rostam Complex (Oedipus Complex in the West). Patriarchal Complex has taken root in our racial subconscious so deeply that it has become a natural trait.

The second way to get famous was to be a member of a

political party, especially the Tudeh Party (pro-Russian
Communist Party in Iran). Then all the authorities and
members of the Party, together with their clandestine or
official publications and their loudspeakers (the radio
broadcasts themselves were made from abroad), applauded
you. "Socialist Realism" was their manifesto in their
writings.

The third way that led to fame was to belong to a clique
or a group of writers. During the reign of the Shah, there
were two groups, each with their own followers. The first
preferred the theory of art for art's sake, and were close to
Romanticism. They were in favor of elaborate prose. The
late Hejazi was their favorite and the late Dashti, who
succeeded him, attracted writers and readers among the
"Bourgeois Compradore," but he soon gave up writing
fiction and turned to academic research, using a powerful
prose. He had been appointed a member of the Senate.

The main current of Persian contemporary literature was
in the hands of the second group. They were widely read
by university students, anti-governmental intellectuals and
the younger generation.

Due to the large number of writers and poets, both men
and women, the diversity of literary genres, and masterpieces produced, the decade of the 1960s was the most
fertile age of Persian literature. Nearly all groups produced
their best.

The intellectual group's fame was not without justifica-
tion, but one cannot categorize them. They had similarities
and differences. The titles attributed to them were more
or less as follows: Modernists, Westernists, Progressivists,
Avant-Garde, Writers Engagés, and artists in favor of the

theory of art for society's sake. Most of them were leftists. I suppose they were revolutionary, politically involved and intellectual artists. They were against the existing conditions and wanted to change them. So they attacked them, some in frank realist prose, close to journalism, while others used similes and metaphors and ended with symbolism. It started with Jamalzadeh, a pioneer as far as form was concerned. He wrote short stories with Western techniques and used colloquial vocabulary in his prose. Then Hedayat followed with a stronger Western technique and more prominent characteristics. His masterpiece, *The Blind Owl*, in fact a masterpiece of modern Persian literature, has a Kafkaesque atmosphere and is inspired by Hinduism. Here he has interwoven dream and fact and has played with both. Later he became an "angry young man," who had every right to be, but he went so far in using colloquial vocabulary that he included obscene words and idioms in his prose. He tried Socialist Realism also, but without success. Hedayat had opened the door for this group, although, his best disciple, Chuback, turned to Naturalism.

In the decade of the 1960s, the idol of the intellectual group was Jalal Al-e Ahmad. Many writers who belonged to this group confessed to me that when they wrote a story, for instance, they asked themselves whether Jalal would like it.

Many thinkers believe that the Iranian Islamic Revolution has been influenced by this group. There is not enough data to judge. I suppose masses followed their religious leaders from the mosques to the streets among whom very few had read a line from the works of these highly intellectual writers. These thinkers believe that the essence of their writing could be felt in the air, and could at least make the younger generation follow the masses with sure steps. The younger generation, yes, but we must not ignore the influence of Dr. Ali Shariati, reconciling the majority of the younger generation to religion with his lectures and religious writings. To attract most of them he had derived some similarity between *Alavi-Shiism* and *Marxism*, and exposed them in his lectures and writings. Sometimes he flirted with Existentialism also. On the whole, fiction was not a literary genre to attract Dr. Shariati or any other religious writer.

There were independent writers besides those I have mentioned. Golestan was the best among them. Some critics have called him a formalist. Formalist or not, his prose is modern and formidable.

There were a few real formalists, who called themselves ultra-modernists and were supported by the court. What they wrote was seldom understood, and I wonder if they understood it themselves. They were soon forgotten. I was close to the intellectual group that had my husband as its leader, and I had many great friends among them. They were welcome in our house, came quite often, and read their stories and poems. Thus I had become completely aware of their prose, poems and ideas.

Having Doctor's degree in Persian literature, I had studied Persian masterpieces, both in prose and poetry. The prose I derived from my studies was not appropriate for writing fiction, and I didn't want to imitate anybody's prose, including my husband's, which was fashionable. It took time, but with enough practice and effort, I achieved a prose that neither continued the traditional nor imitated the Modernists, but which was at the same time nourished by both. The critics have neglected my prose that seems simple, colloquial and idiomatic, but occasionally I use words laden with cultural, philosophical, mystical and even mythological connotations. With those words I make images, trying to come close to poetry. What wonders words are able to perform! So the elite discover the significance of my prose and enjoy it, and the majority of my readers weep or laugh at the destiny of characters I have selected among them. Being a teacher of aesthetics for a long time, I know about "construction" and "harmony" and other aesthetical values.

When Jalal and I decided to marry, my only condition was that "I will remain Simin Daneshvar, not being identified as Mrs. Al-e Ahmad, and thus I would keep my freedom, my philosophical aspects, my ideology, my style of writing . . . and several male friends (not lovers) I have." I didn't predict that we would face such poverty, that I would be forced to translate, in addition to teaching fulltime. In our country nobody can depend on writing to earn a living.

Many political parties tried to persuade me to join them. The late Mr. Maleki, founder of the Third Force Party which later became the "Society of Socialists," insisted that I should become a member, my husband being one of the main sponsors. I answered: "I can't be a political activist, lacking the necessary discipline and devotion, and needing to be open to the world from all directions. I rather prefer to struggle against the despotic, colonialist and male-dominated culture, and to make people aware of their condition, so they won't become the victims of the first

ideology they encounter." Mr. Maleki answered that with
such a government, I couldn't, unless I joined a party,
preferably the Society of Socialists. I answered: "Well sir,
I admire your Humanistic Socialism. I too want all human
beings to equally enjoy the necessary means of a decent and
joyful life, a roof over their heads, clothing, education,
health services, and freedom . . . not being equal in losses
and drawbacks like people of several so-called socialist
countries we know of." But I added, "Where we differ is
that you brought God down from heaven to earth, while I
can't live without metaphysics, metaphysics not according
to the western conception, but my own mystical and
oriental metaphysics."

Then I continued: "God, the source of energy and the
complete energy Himself, is unrecognized, but I see and
feel His manifestations. His manifestations for me include:
love, friendship, hope, freedom, the transcendence that
result from the arts and sciences, the fragrance in flowers,
the growing, the blooming, the light and the ecstasy when
I concentrate on the wonders of creation. But it is in silence
that His voice caresses our senses like a cool breeze on a
hot summer afternoon."

Mr. Maleki smiled and answered that all I saw and felt
belonged to poetry, not to real life which is interwoven
with politics. To rescue myself I joked, "Maybe you
consider God a rightist, and the Devil a leftist," and
concluded that I didn't want to worship the Devil. We both
laughed and our friendship lasted until the end of his life.
His company was a rich sauce that flavored my mind.

To resume my ideas about artistic creation, I can declare
that Capitalism and Socialism are self-centered and

mass-centered, and an artist, being aware of both of them, should stay above them.

The number of different political groups were so many that it made the younger generation dizzy. As a teacher at Tehran University, I noticed how the students shifted from one to the other, and at last most of them, if male, grew beards and, if female, wore scarves. Once with lots of trouble and recommendations I managed to go to Evin prison to visit Dr. Saedi, who had been imprisoned. The tape recorder was running in the office in which we met, and one of the authorities of the SAVAK was present. After swallowing my tears, and talking with Saedi about ordinary things, I complained to our guard of the daily increased number of SAVAK members. I had recognized two SAVAK students in my own class, who had tape recorders and set them running the moment I opened my mouth. He informed me that there were fifty-three different political groups that he knew of, nine of them leftist, from Stalinist-Marxists to Maoists, ending with Islamic Marxists, and he concluded that the religious group and the body of their partisans needed watching. Then he asked me: "What do you say now?" I resumed: "It points out the dizziness of our generation."

How I wanted to open my mouth and tell him what I thought and felt were the reasons—but I didn't. If I had, I would have joined Saedi in Evin Prison. I wanted to tell him: "There are no free elections, no free press, no free political parties, no party clubs where the young can discuss their condition and to what part of the world he or she belongs."

I wanted to say: "Every establishment, every governmental institution, and every decision related to them have been concentrated in the hands of one person—the Shah. Even the two parties get directives from the Dictator, and whenever he decides, he could close them and open another shop," something he later did.

I wanted to ask him: "Who are those whom he respects? To whom does the Shah listen?" And I wanted to answer myself: "To the foreign consultants and advisors, who are scattered in all the key organizations: the army, the petroleum industry, the plan organization, the Ministry of Education, the Ministry of Fine Arts, the Iron Foundry." Because in the beginning of the meeting, he had referred sarcastically to the fact that I taught in the Archaeology Department, and had asked what was the connection between archaeology and the political prisoners that I was so eager to visit, I wanted to tease him and say: "It's been more than a century that foreigners have been interested in our archeology and taken part in our excavations."

I wanted to emphasize: "The only ones who are not worth a damn in the eyes of the Shah are Iranians, as if the Iranian nation did not exist for him."

I had heard from a trusted friend that the Ministry of War had decided to change the buttons of army outfits. The Minister of War took the button selected by the army committee to the Shah for the last decision.

Words and sentences had made a lump in my throat, and I still wanted to say more: to say that even the least important activities were put in the hands of the Queen, and that she was in charge of more than twenty centers, from cancer research centers to art festivals. Although I did not have enough information, I had a mind to think:

how many hours does one have in twenty-four hours, and the Shah, being frail, how could he take on so many responsibilities?

When I am unable, or not permitted, to say what I think and feel, or when I am ignorant of the whole truth, I get sick. Dr. Freud, have you ever encountered such a case?

On my way home, I got lost. I stopped the car several times and asked for directions. Nobody knew. I was caught on a winding road, passed a blind alley and reached the closed door of a garden. The trees were taller than the high walls, and celebrated a farewell party with the sun, which was kissing their shoulders. I stopped and blew my horn. The door opened and a woman with a child in her arms appeared. She pointed out a passage and assured me that it would lead to the highway.

That night I couldn't sleep for a long time, thinking that all of us are wanderers. We all want to do something, but we don't know how, when, and in which direction. So I had better stick to the only work I could do. I decided to write *The Wandering Island*. At least it helped to expose the situation. It is a long novel that is finished now, but there was no paper (except for the very expensive brand on the black market) for it to be printed. In this novel, I combined documentation with imagination.

Our epoch is a bitter one. The world is in turmoil, full of noise and terrorism, full of sex and AIDS, full of narcotics and alcoholism, together with the pollution of the environment, pollution of hands and brains, tensions between East and West, and the threat over our heads of a third World War with modern weapons that could destroy humanity.

Capitalism was not the answer anymore. Marxism, during almost seventy years of experience, showed that it was not the answer either. But there must be another way, a road that leads to the happiness and the comfort of humanity. Philosophy and ideology do not end with Marx, who belonged to the century past.

When I am shivering from the cold, and darkness envelops me due to the scarcity of fuel and electricity brought on by Iraqi bombings of our towns and main centers of energy, I start dreaming about the future. I dream of a universal reconciliation. I dream that all nations have become one state. I dream that all money, wasted on armaments, propaganda, hot and cold wars, is spent for the welfare of humanity. I dream that all the minds from all over the world have been drawn together, led by retired professors in both science and humanities, who can still think and work, and all of them, hand-in-hand, guiding us through wandering paths, blind alleys and winding roads. I dream that they are finding a new and sure highway that leads to the freedom and the well-being of mankind. I have great hope that my dreams will come true, if not for my generation, then for the next.

Simin Daneshvar
Tehran, January 1988

Terracotta female figurine
Iran; 7th century B.C.

Translator's Afterword

Among contemporary writers of Iran, the majority of whom are men, one woman stands out: Simin Daneshvar. Her work has developed and matured since the late 1940s, and today she is known as one of Iran's best fiction writers. Her masterpiece novel *Savushun* (Mourning for Siavash), published in 1969, is considered the climax of Persian novel writing.

Daneshvar, like most contemporary Iranian writers, came from a middle-class family. Born in 1921 in Shiraz, she was educated in a missionary school and became fluent in English. She began her writing career as early as 1935, when she was still an eighth-grader. Her first article, "Winter Is Not Unlike Our Life," was published in a local Shiraz newspaper. She entered Tehran University and majored in Persian literature. When her father, a physician, died in 1941, Daneshvar was forced to find a job, as the family's only source of income had been her father's salary. She was employed at Radio Tehran, where she wrote a series of programs entitled "The Unknown Shirazi," for which she received scant pay. In acute need of money, she even wrote articles on cooking. Eventually, her fluency in English enabled her to become assistant director of foreign news. But she soon became dissatisfied with the routine nature of this job and left Radio Tehran for a newspaper called *Iran*, for which she wrote articles and did translations. The relaxed social and political environment of the forties, marked by some degree of democracy and freedom of speech, prompted Daneshvar to choose journalism as a potential career. During her year at *Iran* (1941-1945), she decided to try her hand at fiction writing. Later, without prior knowledge of story-writing technique, she wrote *Atash-e Khamoush* (The Quenched Fire) in 1948, at the age of twenty-seven. Although seven out of sixteen stories are O. Henry inspired, and Daneshvar had the book published in first draft form, the major elements of her style are evident. Daneshvar had become familiar with O. Henry as a student, and like him she deals with the basic issues of life, death, love and self sacrifice. Typical of writers of the 1940s, Daneshvar dwells on issues within Iranian society. She juxtaposes the opposing values of right and wrong—such as poverty versus wealth, or the carefree life of the rich versus the sorrow of the poor—and for moral reasons condemns one while praising the other. Daneshvar's characters in *The Quenched Fire* are generic types like "professor," "mother," or "daughter," characters without time, place or class who hardly possess a personality.

Her lifelong concern with women and their place in society is apparent in her narrative as early as *The Quenched Fire*. However, at this early stage, Daneshvar does not analyze the socio-economic dependence of women; rather, she is concerned with the general position of women in society. Technically, Daneshvar's major preoccupation at this time was her conscious distinction between the "I" of the author and the "I" of a character. Dual narration in some of her stories made them technically weak.

The Quenched Fire, however, was well received, despite its shortcomings—perhaps because it was the first collection of short stories published by an Iranian woman. Later, Daneshvar refused to have the book reprinted, stating that she would never again turn in a first draft to a publisher. The year following the publication of *The Quenched Fire*, Daneshvar received her Ph.D. in Persian literature from Tehran University. Subsequently, she became acquainted with Jalal Al-e Ahmad, the famous contemporary writer and social critic, during a trip from Isfahan to Tehran. They were married in 1950. Two years later, Daneshvar received a Fulbright scholarship and left for Stanford University for two years. During this time, she published two short stories in English in *The Pacific Spectator*. Upon her return to Iran, she joined Tehran University as an associate professor of art history, a post she held for twenty years. Daneshvar was never granted a professorship—not for the lack of credentials, but due to the influence of SAVAK, the secret police, as she would learn later from the president of the university. She had always been an outspoken and articulate lecturer who believed that her primary responsibility was to her students. Precisely for this reason, she would have many confrontations with the SAVAK throughout her years at the University.

Daneshvar published her second collection of short stories, *Shahri Chon Behesht* (A City as Paradise), in 1961. Meanwhile, her translations of Chekhov, Shaw, Hawthorne, Schnitzler and Saroyan[34] had become a valuable addition to the collection of foreign works available in Persian. In *A City as Paradise*, Daneshvar's prose style had matured considerably, coming closer to the language of the people, no longer as formal as it had been in *The Quenched Fire*. Instead she had developed a short, clear and concise sentence structure. It was from this time onward that she tried to bring her writing closer to cinematographic realism. Her earlier preoccupation with the presence of the "I" of the author is, however, still present in some of the stories in this volume. It is only in *The Playhouse*, the last story, that she finally succeeded in freeing her prose of this distracting element. Her other preoccupation, which began at this stage, is with the concept of time. Similar to Al-e Ahmad and Sa'edi, she felt the need to remind her readers constantly of the passage of time in the form of days, weeks, months or seasons. In *The Accident*, the length of the argument between the husband and wife over the purchase of the car is made clear by: "It took three weeks for me to surrender," or "In three months and eleven days my wife . . ."[35]

---

[34]*The Chocolate Soldier*, by George Bernard Shaw (1949); *The Enemies*, by Antoine Chekov (1952); *Beatrice*, by Arthur Schnitzler (1953); *The Scarlet Letter*, by Nathaniel Hawthorne (1954); *The Human Comedy*, by William Saroyan (1954); *Along With The Sun*, by various authors (1958); *The Best of Chekhov* (1968); and *Cry, the Beloved Country*, by Allen Paton (1972).

[35]Houshang Golshiri, "Jedal-e Naqsh ba Naqash," *Naqd-e Agah* (Spring 1984): 184.

Daneshvar asserted her devotion to recording women's conditions in Iranian society in *A City as Paradise*. Here she no longer dwells on the general characteristics of women; rather, she assumes a neutral position and avoids passing judgement on them; she merely portrays the women and their lives as she saw them. Her characters are able to speak for themselves and demonstrate where their major strengths and weaknesses lie. She is also quite successful in creating the real, as well as the imaginary, worlds of her characters. In *Bibi Shahr Banu*, Daneshvar cleverly depicts the actual lives of her characters, juxtaposed against the lives they wished they could have had. In *The Playhouse*, her handling of Siah's character and his secret love for the girl is subtle, yet far-reaching. In her portrayal of the girl as a victim of society and of her own ignorance, Daneshvar surpasses all of her prior stories.

At the time *A City as Paradise* was published, Daneshvar was still under the shadow of her husband, Al-e Ahmad, who was an imposing figure in Tehran's literary circles.[36] Al-e Ahmad had begun writing in 1945 and by 1961 had published seven novels and short story collections,[37] establishing himself as a notable writer and critic. It was not until the publication of *Savushun*,[38] Daneshvar's masterpiece novel, in 1969, that she attained recognition as an indispensable writer of modern Persian literature, surpassing even Al-e Ahmad in literary importance. *Savushun* was the first novel written by an Iranian woman

---

[36]Ibid. p. 161.

[37]*The Exchange of Visits* (1946), *Our Suffering* (1947), *Sihtar* (1948), *The Unwanted Woman* (1952), *The Tale of the Beehives* (1955), *The School Principal* (1958), *N and the Pen* (1961).

[38]Forthcoming translation in English (Mage Publishers, 1990).

and from a woman's perspective. The book has been reprinted sixteen times and to this date remains the single most widely read Persian novel. In *Savushun* there are no longer traces of weak technique, structure, or style. The story, told from Zari's perspective, depicts a Shirazi landowning family which has become entangled in the dirty politics of the 1940s, instigated by foreign intruders and local opportunists. The hero, Yusuf, Zari's husband, resists the foreigners' demands that he turn over his crop to feed the occupying army. To do so would result in the starvation of his own peasants. He pays for his stubbornness with his life. The last scene of the novel is that of Yusuf's burial procession, which is on the verge of turning into a mass demonstration. However, government troops disperse the demonstrators, leaving his body to be carried by his brother and Zari. This scene is among the most moving and well written passages in Persian literature. In *Savushun*, Daneshvar integrates social events, traditional customs, and beliefs, creating a beautifully narrated story.

Daneshvar's husband died a few months before the publication of *Savushun*. After Al-e Ahmad's death, Daneshvar continued her involvement in the activities that had been important to her husband. She assumed a leading role in the Writers' Association, which Al-e Ahmad had helped to found, encouraging young writers in their efforts. In her understated yet resolute way, she provided moral support for intellectuals and dissidents opposing the Pahlavi regime. She specifically concentrated her efforts on assisting her students financially and academically. When she refers to political issues in her writings, it is within the broad context of unjust political systems, for Daneshvar never adhered to a particular political ideology.

During the mid-1970s Daneshvar kept a low profile. She maintained her position as associate professor and became the chairman of the Department of Art History and Archaeology. In addition to her work at the University, she wrote a series of short stories. A few of these were published in magazines and finally compiled in 1980. *To Whom Can I Say Hello?* established Daneshvar as a good short story writer, as well as an able novelist. In the stories *Traitor's Intrigue*, *To Whom Can I Say Hello?*, and *The Accident*, Daneshvar upholds the standards of excellence she had attained in *Savushun*. In this last collection, Daneshvar expands her earlier convictions. The diversity of her characters and her choice of themes reflect her thorough understanding of the multi-faceted Iranian society. She captures the mentality, the ideals, aspirations, lifestyles, manner of speech, and popular expressions of Iran's various social strata. Her well-rounded characters are representative of their time and place, presenting a colorful view of Iranian behavior. This quality in her writing affirms the faithfulness of her work as being a true mirror of society.

Daneshvar's stories reflect reality rather than fantasy. They contain themes such as child theft, adultery, marriage, childbirth, sickness, death, treason, profiteering, illiteracy, ignorance, poverty and loneliness. The issues she deals with are the social problems of the 1960s and 1970s, which have immediacy and credibility for the reader. Her inspiration is drawn from the people around her. In her own words: "Simple people have much to offer. They must be able to give freely and with piece of mind. We, too, in return, must give to them to the best of our abilities.

We must, with all our heart, try to help them acquire what they truly deserve."[39]

Daneshvar depicts the lifestyles of the lower classes, the traditional middle class, and the bourgeoisie with equal clarity. Through her characters one becomes familiar with these various classes. A few examples will help illustrate the diversity of her female characters. Nadia in *The Accident* is a bourgeois woman who sacrifices her marriage (and potentially the happiness of her children) to further her desired social image. On the other hand, Zari in *Savushun* is a traditional middle class, educated woman from a feudal family. She nobly accepts her husband's self-sacrifice, devoting herself to carry forth his principles of justice and humanity. In contrast, the protagonist in another story, *Anis*, is a lower middle class woman with aspirations of social mobility. A maid who has come from a village to Tehran, she is impressed by the bourgeois lifestyle. Seeking to emulate it, she abandons her self respect, individuality, and economic independence. Marmar in *Vakil Bazaar* is a careless maid who foolishly loses her master's daughter because she cannot tear herself away from a shopkeeper's flirtations. Daneshvar does a brilliant job reproducing Marmar's language. The expressions and idioms Marmar uses are common among the women of her class. Bridging the gap between the spoken and written language has been a major preoccupation of contemporary Persian writers. It is mainly through dialogue that a writer can exercise this practice. Daneshvar, however, is successful in reproducing the cadence of spoken language throughout the whole text

---

[39]Interview with Maryam Mafi, Tehran, Iran, April 1977.

not merely in the dialogue.

Daneshvar is particularly concerned with elderly single women who have worked their entire lives to earn a living, but find themselves poor and broken-hearted in their final years. In *To Whom Can I Say Hello?* Daneshvar sympathetically depicts Kokab Sultan, a hard-working woman who raises her daughter with great difficulty. Having devoted herself to creating the best possible life for her child, she is forced to sell her daughter into marriage when her only source of income is taken away. Daneshvar, who has adopted the plight of the lower classes, especially that of poor women, considers their economic dependence on men as the source of all their misfortune. She largely blames the structure of society for this condition. Muhtaram, the daughter of a poor cobbler in *The Man Who Never Came Back*, marries Ebrahim, a peddler. She is so thrilled with the few extra material things she finds at her husband's house that she does not realize that she is still living in poverty. She becomes aware of the desperation of her situation one day when Ebrahim does not return home. Left with little money, no skills, and two small children, she is forced to acknowledge her complete dependance on her husband. This time, though, Muhtaram is lucky and Ebrahim returns home unharmed, saving them from starvation.

Although Daneshvar underscores the social factors contributing to the unfortunate situation of women, she nevertheless maintains her objectivity, at times turning her critical eye upon the individual. Her characters provide role models that are both positive (Zari in *Savushun*, Maryam in *Bibi Shahr Banu*, Kokab Sultan in *To Whom Can*

I Say Hello?), as well as negative (Nadia in *The Accident*, Anis in *Anis*, the girl in *The Playhouse*). Out of the changing social milieu of the 1960s and 1970s, writers found it far more difficult to develop believable, progressive characters than to recreate negative characters that were easy to mock. For instance, in *The Traitor's Intrigue*, one observes the colonel's character development. An unsympathetic character at the start, he evolves into a positive model by the end of the story. He finally stands on his own two feet, asserting his individuality in the face of the regime, disrupting the old order.

Folklore and traditional Persian customs preoccupied writers in the 1960s and 1970s. Much of Daneshvar's work encompassed traditional customs and rituals. She reminds the reader of the virtues and vices of such traditions. Her fiction details superstitions that have survived for centuries, embedded in the extreme religiosity of the lower classes. The common practices of casting away evil spirits and unlocking misfortunes by resorting to magical prayers and witchcraft appear again and again in her stories. Kokab Sultan in *To Whom Can I Say Hello?* wants to learn the infamy prayer so that she can curse her son-in-law and win her daughter back. The family of the mullah in the *Vakil Bazaar* want to save their son from the evil spirit which has taken over his body by exorcising him, and offering ablutions and prayers. Daneshvar has no qualms with traditional religious ceremonies and rituals like visiting holy shrines, baking *Nazri* (an offering of food to the poor), and performing the daily prayers. She does, however, oppose religious superstition, which can brutalize people's lives.

In 1979, Daneshvar retired from her post at the University, and in the following year published *To Whom Can I Say Hello?* In 1981, she completed a monograph on Al-e Ahmad, *Ghoroub-e Jalal* (The Loss of Jalal). This is the most moving piece she has written, as well as the best descriptive work on the personality of one of Iran's literary leaders. Daneshvar relates her last days with Al-e Ahmad with great detail and emotional understanding. Her prose is formal, proving her mastery of Persian classical literature. Daneshvar currently resides in Tehran and has recently completed a new novel, *Jazireh-ye Sargardani* (The Wandering Island).

Until the appearance of Daneshvar, contemporary Persian literature could boast of only two able women writers—Parvin E'tesami and Forough Farrokhzad—both poets. Daneshvar proved that women could also achieve excellence in prose. Her works stand as precious contributions to the world of fiction in Iran. As a woman and as a writer, she is a model of the up-and-coming women authors who want to address social concerns. Persian literature today has considerable value, especially when viewed as a mirror of society as well as a medium to influence it. Contemporary Iranian writers like Daneshvar have taken it upon themselves to create a link between literature and social change.

A NOTE ABOUT THE AUTHOR

SIMIN DANESHVAR was born in 1921 in Shiraz, Iran, and received her Ph.D. in Persian literature from Tehran University. She has published thirty-six short stories and a major best-selling novel, Savushun, in Persian. She lives and writes in Tehran.

TRANSLATOR'S ACKNOWLEDGMENTS

I would like to thank Dianne McCree and Melissa Vaughn for their endless support, encouragement, and very special editing collaborations.

I would also like to thank Myra Sclarewe, whose inspiring zest for foreign literatures and her uncompromising impetus convinced me of the necessity of translations in order to bridge gaps of different cultures.

Last but not least, I would like to offer my special thanks to both Dr. Daneshvar and Dr. Herdeck for trusting me and believing that I would not let them down.

MARYAM MAFI is a graduate of Tufts University and The American University. She lives in London and is working on an anthology of Persian women writers.

COLOPHON

Type composed in-house by Gerry Cervenka and output through the Linotronic 300 by Versources, Inc.
Printed and bound by Cushing-Malloy
Ann Arbor, Michigan

خوشنویسی کتاب توسط امیر حسین تابناک

Design by Najmieh Batmanglij

DUE DATE

OCT 2 6 2005			
			Printed in USA